'Tis the Season

'Tis the Season

Ann M. Martin

SCHOLASTIC INC.

New York   Toronto   London   Auckland   Sydney
Mexico City   New Delhi   Hong Kong   Buenos Aires

No part of this publication may be reproduced, or stored in a retrieval system, or transmitted in any form or by any means, electronic, mechanical, photocopying, recording, or otherwise, without written permission of the publisher. For information regarding permission, write to Permissions Department, Scholastic Inc., 557 Broadway, New York, NY 10012.

ISBN-13: 978-0-439-86881-5
ISBN-10: 0-439-86881-5

Illustrations by Dan Andreason

Copyright © 2007 by Ann M. Martin. All rights reserved. Published by Scholastic Inc. SCHOLASTIC and associated logos are trademarks and/or registered trademarks of Scholastic Inc.

12 11 10 9 8 7 6 5 4 3 2   7 8 9 10 11 12/0

Printed in the U.S.A.   23

First printing, October 2007

For BH and LH

CHAPTER I

Nikki's News

"All of a sudden it's Christmas!" exclaimed Flora.

Flora and Ruby Northrop had turned left at the end of their block on Aiken Avenue, walked for one block along Dodds Lane, and turned right on Main Street. Even though this was something the girls did many times each week, Flora now came to a halt and stared straight ahead in wonder.

Ruby, two years younger than Flora, let out a squeak of excitement. "It *is* Christmas!" she said.

Main Street in Camden Falls, Massachusetts, was always an interesting place. Picturesque, too. That was what the tourists said. In spring, the forsythia bushes bloomed yellow and the crab apple trees bloomed pink, making Main Street look, Ruby once said, like a bowl of sherbet. In summer, the trees that lined the street were heavy with green leaves and

1

seedpods. In autumn, the maple trees glowed red and orange and gold. Later, when they lost their finery, the stores made up for it. Their owners decorated the doors and windows with lights and pumpkins and sheaves of corn and wreaths of dried flowers.

But this — this was something different.

"It's like a Christmas village. Like one of those little towns you see in magazines," said Flora.

"Why didn't Min tell us this would happen?" asked Ruby.

Thanksgiving, the first Thanksgiving Flora and Ruby had spent in Camden Falls, was just two days behind them, and in that short space of time, Main Street had been transformed.

"Maybe she wanted to surprise us," replied Flora. "I don't know. But it doesn't matter. Look, Ruby. Look at everything."

As Flora and Ruby walked past Dutch Haus and Verbeyst's on their way to Needle and Thread, they gazed up and down the street. Rarely had they seen so much activity. Mr. Freedly, who worked in the new grocery store outside of town, was busy hanging a red-ribboned wreath on each lamppost. Flora could see that he was making his way from the south end of town to the north. Already, eight wreaths had been hung.

"Hi, Mr. Freedly!" called Ruby.

Mr. Freedly looked down from the top of his ladder. "Hello there, Ruby. Hi, Flora."

"Do you do this every year?" asked Ruby.

"What's that?"

"Do you hang these wreaths every single year?"

"Been doing it for more than sixty years now," said Mr. Freedly. "Not me *personally*," he added. "We all take turns. It's a Camden Falls tradition." He paused, fumbling with nails and a loop of wire. "This is your first Christmas here, isn't it, girls?"

"Everything here will be our firsts until June," replied Flora. "Then we'll begin our seconds."

"And nothing will be new anymore," added Ruby.

"Well, I hope that's not true," said Mr. Freedly. "There are always new things."

Flora and Ruby continued their way down Main Street.

"Let's look around a little more before we go to Needle and Thread," said Flora. "Min won't mind. She just said to come before lunchtime."

The girls gawked outside of Frank's Beans, where Frank himself was outlining the windows of his coffee shop with tiny gold lights. Flora could see that the windows of the used bookstore next door had already been outlined. And next door to the bookstore, even the window of Dr. Malone's dental office was strung with lights.

"My stars," said Flora, in exactly the same tone of voice that her grandmother Min used.

Frank poked his head out the door and smiled at her. "What do you think?" he asked.

"Main Street looks . . . I've never seen anything like it."

"Wait until everyone decorates their windows," said Frank. "This is just the beginning. What are your grandmother and Mrs. Walter going to do at Needle and Thread?"

Flora and Ruby looked at each other. "I don't know," said Flora.

"Maybe we should go see," said Ruby.

The girls crossed the street, then ran to Needle and Thread. They burst through the door.

"Min! You didn't tell us what town would look like!" cried Ruby, just as Flora said, "Can we help you decorate the window?"

Min was showing a customer the book of smocking patterns. She held up a finger to the girls, then said to the customer, "Picture patterns are in the front of the book, geometric patterns in the back."

Flora and Ruby flopped onto the couches at the front of the store, the couches on which Camden Falls shoppers sat when they dropped by for a chat-and-stitch. Flora remembered the day last June (was it really just five months ago?) when she and Ruby had come to Needle and Thread for the first time since moving to Camden Falls. Flora was ten then, and Ruby was eight, and everything had seemed foreign and somehow distant, even the store, which of course they had visited before. Now Needle and Thread was as familiar as any room in their house.

"Flora?" said Ruby from her spot on the couch. She fingered a button she'd found on the coffee table. "Are you sorry we came to Camden Falls?"

Flora sighed. Why did Ruby have to ask questions that were so complicated? Flora was certainly sorry about the *reason* they had moved to Camden Falls. If there were a way, some magical way, in which she could reverse time and travel back to that snowy January night, she would surely try to do something to prevent the accident that had taken the lives of their parents. But the accident had happened, and a lot of other things had happened after that. Their energetic grandmother Min (short not for Mindy, which was her name, but for "In a minute," which Min used to say all the time) had temporarily left her quiet life in Camden Falls to move in with Flora and Ruby, to take care of them and comfort them. Then Min had sold the house in which Flora and Ruby had grown up and moved them back to Camden Falls — to the house in which their own mother had grown up. The girls had settled in at their new school and some things were very, very good. Their new friends Olivia and Nikki, for instance. And Needle and Thread. Flora loved to sew, and spending so much time in a sewing store was a dream come true. Ruby, who planned on becoming a star of some sort, was a member of the Camden Falls Children's Chorus. And she took dance lessons. And she had the lead in the school play. If Flora and Ruby had to become orphans, this wasn't a bad way to do it.

So, no, Flora wasn't exactly sorry she had come to Camden Falls. But was she sorry about the accident, and did she miss her parents and her old friends and her old life? Of course.

Flora turned to Ruby to try to explain all this and saw that Ruby had already lost interest and was talking to Gigi, behind the counter. Gigi, whose real name was Mrs. Evelyn Walter, was Min's friend and business partner. Min and Gigi had owned and run Needle and Thread for years. Gigi's granddaughter Olivia lived next door to Min and Flora and Ruby in the Row Houses, and Olivia, one year younger than Flora but in her sixth-grade class because she was smart and had skipped a grade, had become one of Flora and Ruby's best friends. That was another nice thing about Camden Falls: having a best friend right next door.

"Flora!" Ruby called then. "Gigi said we can decorate the window. She did! And she said Olivia's on her way over, so she can help us."

Flora's heart skipped a little. There was nothing she liked better than starting a new project, especially a creative one. And dressing the store window sounded rather important and grown-up.

"Can we do whatever we want?" asked Flora, joining Ruby and Gigi behind the checkout counter.

"Well," said Gigi, "Min and I decided we want a winter scene for the window. We have some blue fabric for sky, a lot of cotton batting for snow, and some cardboard and sparkles for making snowflakes. But you can make whatever kind of winter scene you want."

Gigi helped Flora and Ruby carry the box of supplies to the window. The last time Flora had seen the window, the backdrop was of falling autumn leaves. In the front, gourds and pumpkins tumbled across a bed of straw. And to one side stood a scarecrow that Flora, Ruby, Olivia, and Nikki had made and dressed in old clothes. Now the window was bare.

"It's all yours," said Gigi, setting down an armload of tiny electric lights and a box of glittery yellow stars.

Gigi retreated into the store, followed by Ruby. Flora sat down in the center of the empty window and looked out at Main Street. Shoppers hurried by just inches from her nose, separated only by the pane of glass. Some of them paid her no notice, but a few glanced over their shoulders in surprise when they realized that a live girl was sitting in the window of the sewing store.

Flora saw old Mrs. Grindle leave Stuff 'n' Nonsense across the street and hurry down the block, probably to Frank's Beans for a cup of coffee. Flora tried hard to like Mrs. Grindle, but Mrs. Grindle was crabby and had once been very mean to Nikki. Flora just couldn't get over it.

Flora looked to her right and there was Sonny Sutphin edging along the sidewalk in his wheelchair, as he did nearly every day. Flora wondered what Sonny did when snow was on the ground, which was bound to be the case soon. Min said Camden Falls got a lot of snow in the winter.

Flora checked her watch and calculated the hours until Mary Woolsey would arrive. She had realized the most amazing thing on Thanksgiving night just as she was falling asleep, and now she couldn't wait until Mary came to work so she could tell her the news.

Flora was still sitting in the window, lost in thought, when Olivia bounced by. Olivia, it seemed, was always in motion. She grinned when she caught sight of Flora in the window, and Flora grinned back. Moments later, Flora, Ruby, and Olivia were examining the decorations.

"I know what we could do!" exclaimed Flora. "We could use the batting for snow, like Gigi said, and in the center of it we could make a frozen pond."

"A frozen pond? Out of what?" asked Ruby.

"A mirror!" said Flora triumphantly.

"Oh, excellent," said Olivia. "And you know what? We could get some china animals from Stuff 'n' Nonsense and put them in the snow and around the pond. It could be a winter woodland scene."

"We could make fir trees," said Ruby.

"And we'll use the blue fabric for the evening sky and hang the stars on it."

"Gigi wanted big snowflakes, I think," said Ruby.

"We could stick them all along the edges of the window," said Olivia. "That would look nice with the lights around the window on the outside. Very glittery and twinkly."

The girls set to work at the table in the front of the store. They began to make the snowflakes first. Nobody wanted to go across the street to buy the animals from Mrs. Grindle.

"Ruby," said Olivia. "Your china animal collection. Could —"

"No way!" cried Ruby. "My animals are special. You can't take them out of their family groupings."

"Well, then, will you be the one to go to Mrs. Grindle's?"

"No."

"My mother started working there yesterday," said Olivia.

"At Stuff 'n' Nonsense?" said Flora, surprised.

"Yup. She's going to be there part-time during the holidays, when the store is extra busy. She needs the work." Olivia's parents had been out of work for several months.

The girls bent over the coffee table, busy with their scissors and cardboard and glue and glitter, until they heard someone say, "Hey, what are you making?"

"Nikki!" said Flora. "I didn't even hear you come in."

Olivia and Ruby and Flora told Nikki their idea for the window, while Nikki settled herself on the couch, saying nothing and staring out the window.

"Don't you want to help us?" Olivia asked her.

"Sorry," Nikki said. "I was just thinking. You guys won't believe what happened last night."

Flora set down her snowflake. "What?" she said.

"Well . . ." Nikki drew the word out, and Flora couldn't tell whether she looked happy or upset. "Well, my father said he's going away for a while. We were all sitting in the kitchen, having supper, and he told us he's taken this construction job somewhere down south where it's warmer, and that he's going to be gone for several months."

"Even for Christmas?" said Ruby, eyes wide.

Nikki nodded. "He said he'll be sending money home while he's away, but that he won't be back until the spring."

"Wow," said Olivia, and she set down her snowflake, too. "Are you . . ." She hesitated. "Are you worried?"

Olivia was careful not to ask whether Nikki was sad, since the girls knew how Nikki felt about her father. Mr. Sherman had an unfortunate reputation in Camden Falls and an even worse one where his family was concerned. All the Shermans — Nikki, Mrs. Sherman, Tobias (Nikki's older brother), and Mae (her little sister) — were afraid of him. Although recently

Tobias had begun to stand up to his father, which Flora knew Nikki found almost as frightening as her father.

Mr. Sherman drank too much. He had a horrible temper. He threw things and he broke things. He was loud and unpredictable. He was never able to hold down a job for more than a week or two. So was Nikki sorry he would be leaving for a few months? No, she was not. But was she worried?

Nikki chose her words carefully. At last she said, "I'm worried that he won't actually send us any money."

"What do you mean?" asked Ruby.

"I mean . . . this all just sounds so, I don't know, so old-fashioned. Like something that would happen in a story about the nineteen thirties. You know *The Journey of Natty Gann*? When Natty's father has to find work during the Depression, and he leaves Natty behind while he looks for a job in a different city? It sounds like that. Romantic, but not quite real. 'Good-bye, kids. I've found work in the South. I'll send you money when I get my first paycheck.' Come on. We don't even know exactly where he's going. You have to admit it's a little strange."

Olivia nodded. "My parents have been out of work for a while now, but they're just looking for jobs here. They're sure something will turn up."

"What about the money?" asked Ruby again.

"Oh," said Nikki. "Well, you know my father. I mean, you know about him." (Flora, Ruby, and Olivia had never actually met Mr. Sherman.) "Would *you* trust him to send money? I don't think so. So I don't think we're going to see a penny. I also don't think he's leaving because he found a job."

Three heads swiveled in Nikki's direction, and Flora raised her eyebrows. "What's he doing, then?"

Nikki shrugged. "He probably just wants to leave us. Go off on his own. Start over without a family. Just have himself to worry about." She paused. "I don't care."

"Nikki, we're your friends," said Olivia. "You can say what you really feel."

"That's what I really feel. I don't care if he wants to get away from us. I'll just be relieved when he's gone." She leaned forward. "Okay. Show me what we're doing here. Do you want me to work on snowflakes?"

Flora and Olivia glanced at each other. Then Olivia took charge. "Sure. Okay. You work on snowflakes. Flora, you can help me hang the fabric for the sky and put the stars on it. Ruby, you run across the street to Mrs. Grindle's."

"Nice try," said Ruby.

"Oh, all right. I'll go," said Olivia. "I'm sure it will be okay. What could happen to me when Mom is there?"

"You never know," said Ruby darkly.

CHAPTER 2

Christmas Is Coming

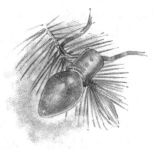

The first time Flora had heard of Mary Woolsey was the day after Flora and Ruby had moved to Camden Falls. King Comma, their cat, had escaped, and Olivia had helped Flora search through half the town before King was discovered in Mr. Pennington's garage. Among the places they had seen as they hunted and called was a tiny, tidy house surrounded by gardens that, to Flora's surprise, Olivia had said was owned by a crazy old lady known as Scary Mary. Olivia had added that Mary was a recluse and that there were all sorts of horrifying stories about her. Just when Flora was thoroughly frightened, Olivia had stunned her by informing her that Scary Mary worked at Needle and Thread. Mary knew Min and Gigi, and they had offered her a job at the store, doing mending and altering and special sewing for N&T customers.

That was way back in June when everything about Camden Falls had been new to Flora. Now when she thought about the tales Olivia had told her she almost laughed. Olivia still believed them, but not Flora. Flora had come to know Mary, and in a way that was most surprising. She had found a photo of her mother at age four posing with a woman who, Flora eventually realized, was a much younger Mary Woolsey. That photo had led to a friendship between Flora and Mary — and to a mystery. Mary told Flora that the photo had been taken years and years earlier when she had visited Min's house looking for Lyman Davis, Min's father (Flora's great-grandfather). She believed he had been the benefactor who had sent her anonymous gifts of money since she was a little girl. On one of the cozy afternoons she and Flora had spent in the little house this fall, Mary had revealed that decades earlier, Lyman Davis had inadvertently been responsible for Mary's parents' losing all their money, which in turn had led to her father's taking a job in a factory that burned down. At the end of that awful, memorable day, Mary's father was one of the factory workers who didn't return home. (It was a complicated story.) Not long after that, the gifts of money started to arrive, but it wasn't until Mary was a grown woman looking through old family papers that it suddenly occurred to her who her benefactor must be. The gifts of money, which had allowed

Mary to live a reasonably comfortable life, continued to arrive throughout the years until 1966, when Mary was thirty-six years old.

This was all well and good — a neat and tidy story, thought Flora — except for one thing. On this past Thanksgiving night, in a conversation with Min, Flora had learned that her great-grandfather had died in 1964. So how had Mary continued to receive the gifts for two years after Lyman Davis's death? There was only one way that could have happened: All those years the money must have been sent by someone other than Flora's great-grandfather. But who? Flora's heart started to pound just thinking about this.

That afternoon, as she and Ruby and Nikki and Olivia worked away at their window (the trip to Mrs. Grindle's had been uneventful, since the store had been crowded and Olivia had made a beeline for her mother), Flora kept looking at the clock, waiting for Mary Woolsey to arrive. When at last she walked through the door of Needle and Thread, Flora leaped to her feet, a shower of paper scraps and glitter falling from her lap.

"Mary!" she cried. "Mary, I have to tell you something."

Mary, startled, looked at the four girls working at the table by the window. She saw one shiny brown face, two shiny pink faces, and Nikki's faintly smudged face. (Hot water was sometimes in short supply at the Shermans'.) "Yes?" she said, edging toward her work space at the back of the store.

Flora followed her. "Mary," she said again, "my great-grandfather died in nineteen sixty-four. Min told me so."

Mary shrugged out of her coat and hung it on the back of her chair. She turned to Flora, frowning.

"Well, don't you see?" Flora went on. "You said you got the last envelope of money in nineteen sixty-six. Lyman Davis had been dead for two years then."

"Well, my word," said Mary. And then, "My *word*."

"It's a mystery, isn't it?" said Flora.

"It is indeed. A real mystery."

"Unless Min's *mother* had been sending the money all along," said Flora, hoping desperately that Mary wouldn't agree with her. She liked the idea of a mystery.

Mary looked thoughtful, but then she shook her head. "I don't know, of course, but I really don't think so. Mrs. Davis was a very nice lady, but she didn't have the . . ." Mary paused, thinking, "the *guilt* that your great-grandfather did. She wasn't the one who lost my parents' nest egg; she wasn't the one who fired my mother. It would take a good, solid, strong reason to send so much money for so many years. Mrs. Davis didn't have such a reason."

"So who did," asked Flora, "if it wasn't my great-grandfather?"

"I have no idea," Mary replied. "No idea at all."

Flora spent the rest of the busy day wrapped in delicious mysterious feelings as well as delicious Christmasy ones. "I've never seen Camden Falls so crowded," she said to Olivia.

"This is what always happens after Thanksgiving. It's the holiday rush."

The window still wasn't finished when Min asked Flora if she would run to the copy center for her. Flora did so, not pausing to chat with Mr. Adams, who was working at the counter. She returned just as Gigi asked Olivia to run across the street to Stuff 'n' Nonsense again, this time to borrow Mrs. Grindle's hammer. "I can't imagine what happened to ours," said Gigi.

As Olivia ran by Flora, she whispered, "No way am I asking the Grinch for the hammer. I hope Mom knows where it is."

Flora had just settled down next to Nikki again when the door to Needle and Thread opened and in walked Mr. and Mrs. Fong, who lived at one end of the Row Houses. Mrs. Fong's hand was resting on her belly, which was starting to look rather big.

"Hi!" Flora said, happy to see them.

"Hello, Flora," replied Mr. Fong, and Mrs. Fong smiled and said, "We thought it was time to begin making some things for the baby's room."

Flora grinned. "We have a lot of really great stuff for kids. You could start over there with that rack labeled 'Juvenile Fabrics.' You might want to look at the flannels, too. We have a selection of flame-retardant flannels. What are you going to make?"

"We're not sure yet," replied Mrs. Fong.

"We have a lot of ideas," added her husband. "Curtains, bumpers for the crib."

"Maybe a seat cushion for the rocking chair," said Mrs. Fong.

"Do you know whether the baby is a boy or a girl?" asked Flora.

"Nope," said Mrs. Fong. "But we're going to find out soon."

Flora showed the Fongs the interior decor sections in the books of sewing patterns and was about to join Nikki again when she glanced outside and saw Sonny in his wheelchair. He was sitting by the door, facing Main Street. Flora poured a cup of coffee from the pot Min and Gigi kept going for the chat-and-stitchers and brought it to Sonny.

"Thank you, Flora," said Sonny, taking it in his good hand.

"It's kind of chilly today," said Flora.

"Snow's in the air. I can smell it."

"Really?" Flora asked. "When is it coming?"

"Don't know for sure, but it's around the corner."

Flora wondered for the millionth time about Sonny Sutphin's life before she had met him. It was strange to know absolutely nothing about a person's background. She knew at least a little about most of her new friends in Camden Falls — Nikki, Mary Woolsey, her Row House neighbors. But not Sonny. And she didn't feel comfortable asking him questions. For instance, right now she wanted to say to Sonny, "What will you do after it snows? Can you get around in your wheelchair? Why do you need the wheelchair in the first place? What holidays do you celebrate? Do you celebrate with anyone? Do you have a family?" She thought she knew the answers to some of the questions, but she would have liked to hear them from Sonny himself.

Now, as Sonny sipped the coffee, he said to her, "You're going to catch cold, Flora, standing out here with no coat. Thank you for the coffee, but you'd better go back inside. I'll leave the mug on the bench when I'm finished."

It wasn't until darkness was falling that Flora realized there was a lull in all the activity. Only one customer was wandering around Needle and Thread, and the door hadn't opened or closed in ten minutes. Min and Gigi looked at each other, and Min said, "My land, let's sit down for a bit."

"Girls, you are doing a wonderful job," said Gigi,

settling herself onto the couch and watching the progress in the window.

"Thank you," said Nikki.

And Ruby added, "We're almost done. We can probably finish tomorrow."

"Hey, Gigi," said Olivia, "are we going to have those gift workshops again this year?"

"What gift workshops?" asked Flora.

"In December we usually have workshops at the store to make presents for people who might not get any other presents at the holidays," Olivia explained.

"They're distributed with the Special Delivery meals at Christmas and Hanukkah," added Min.

Flora nodded. She knew about Special Delivery. Her neighbor Mr. Pennington had a Special Delivery route, taking cooked meals to homebound Camden Falls residents.

"What presents do you make?" asked Ruby.

"Well," said Olivia, "we supply fabric and buttons and trims, and people stop by all day to make eyeglass cases, pillows, aprons, fleece scarves, that kind of thing. It's really fun."

"Our customers bring cookies and candy and even eggnog," added Min. "It's like a party."

"Excellent!" said Ruby.

"So are we going to have the workshops this year?" asked Flora.

"Yes," replied Min. "Two, I think."

"One during the week, and one on a Saturday," added Gigi.

"Goody," said Ruby. "We can all come to the Saturday workshop."

"All right," said Min. "Time to close up the store."

Ruby looked at the clock. "Now? But it's only quarter to five."

"And that's the perfect time for the lighting of the Main Street Christmas tree."

Outside Flora could see that the street was even more crowded than before. People were streaming by Needle and Thread, all hurrying in the same direction.

Olivia was grinning. "This is almost as good as what happens on Christmas Eve. You didn't know about this, did you?" she said to Flora and Ruby.

They shook their heads.

And Nikki added, "I've heard about it, but I've never seen it."

"You're kidding," said Olivia. "I thought you lived here all your life."

"I have. But we never came into town for this. In fact," Nikki went on, looking worried, "I probably shouldn't be here now. I think I was supposed to go home before it got dark. I wasn't paying attention."

"Call your parents," said Gigi gently. "Tell them I'll drive you home as soon as the tree has been lit."

Nikki, hands shaking, used the phone at the checkout counter to call her house. "I think the service has been turned off again," she said a minute later.

Gigi put an arm around her. "This is not for you to worry about. Come with us and enjoy the ceremony. Min and I will take care of things."

"Okay. Thank you," said Nikki.

Min was walking around the store, turning off sewing machines and unplugging irons and the coffeepot. "Will you join us, Mary?" she said as Mary slipped into her coat.

Mary bowed her head. "I think I'll head on home."

Even Flora knew better than to beg her to stay. But she did say, "I'll see you next week. Keep thinking about our mystery!"

At last, the store lights were turned off, too, except for the tiny gold ones that now bordered the window, and Min, Gigi, Flora, Ruby, Olivia, and Nikki stepped into the frosty night air. They joined the crowd moving along the sidewalk, sleeves brushing sleeves, mittened hands raised in greetings, boots tromping. Every business had closed, Flora realized, but the streetlights glowed, and the windows were alive with mechanical Santas and trimmed trees and glowing stars. Flora passed several menorahs, the candles still unlit as the first night of Hanukkah was two weeks away. As she paused by some windows, she heard music — songs and carols and bells chiming — and as she paused by others, she smelled chocolate and cider and warm buttery things.

"Ooh, look!" Ruby said suddenly.

They had reached the town square. A fir tree, at least three stories high, had been placed in the center of the square. Its branches were dark, but Flora could see the lights that had been twined around them, and she could smell the sharp scent that made her feel as if she were deep in a pine forest. In front of the tree a group of carolers, each holding a candle, stood in a tight knot, voices raised. "*Adeste fideles!*" they sang.

"'Everywhere, everywhere, Christmas tonight,'" murmured Flora, remembering a poem she had once read.

And at that, Nikki cried out, "Mom!" She broke away from Flora and Ruby and Olivia and wiggled through the crowd of people.

"Hey, there's Mae," said Olivia, pointing to Nikki's little sister.

"And Tobias," added Flora.

"And I guess that's Mrs. Sherman," said Ruby.

The carolers stopped singing then, and one of them stepped forward and led the crowd in "Deck the Halls" and "Silent Night." There was a moment of expectant silence, and then a tree of blue and green and gold and red and violet and white sprang forth from the darkness.

Flora drew in her breath. It's like magic, she

thought. But years later, even when she was a grown woman remembering this Christmas in Camden Falls, the image that would first come into her mind was not of the tree but of Nikki standing between her mother and Mae, holding their hands, Tobias behind them, their faces shining, Mae's nearly awestruck.

Flora didn't know why Mrs. Sherman, who never attended town events, had decided to come to the lighting of the tree but she thought perhaps she had been emboldened by the thought of a life without Mr. Sherman. Flora took this as a very good sign.

Everyone admired the tree for a few minutes ("It will stay lit until New Year's Day," said Min), and then they began to drift away.

"Good-bye!" Flora and Olivia and Ruby called to Nikki.

Gigi and Olivia's grandfather walked to their car. Olivia had found her parents and her brothers and also Mr. Pennington, who lived next door to her, and they made their way back to the Row Houses with Min, Ruby, and Flora, turning left off Main Street onto Dodds Lane, then right onto Aiken Avenue. And there before Flora were the Row Houses, looking in the dark like a castle. They were actually eight attached houses that had been built in 1882, and they were the only ones of their kind in Camden Falls. Flora had already begun to think of the Row House residents, all twenty-five of them, as her very large family. She passed by first the Morrises' house, dark since the Morrises had gone away for Thanksgiving; then by the Willets' house, where Mr. and Mrs. Willet were probably eating supper; and then by the Malones' house, which was also dark, before turning onto their walk.

"See you tomorrow!" Flora called to Olivia as the Walters turned onto their own walk next door.

From down the dimly lit street she heard Mr. Pennington and Robby Edwards and his parents and the Fongs calling good-bye and good night to one another. Ruby opened their front door and Min grabbed the mail from the letter box. She stood in the front hallway and leafed through the envelopes as Daisy Dear galumphed out of the kitchen and King Comma made a more subtle appearance.

"Huh," said Min, an open card in her hand. "This is from your aunt Allie, girls. She says she's planning to visit at Christmas and that she'll call soon to make arrangements. My stars. She hasn't visited Camden Falls in years."

This turned out to be bigger news than Flora could have imagined.

CHAPTER 3

Camden Falls Elementary

Nicolette Sherman didn't usually wake up cheerful, but on Monday morning she woke up feeling as though she could whistle and skip and dance all day long. Who cared if it was raining? Who cared if it was Monday? Who cared if Thanksgiving vacation had ended? Who cared if Mr. Donaldson, her new teacher, was taking over today, and Mrs. Mandel, her favorite teacher ever, had left? The day before, her father had packed up his clothes and a few belongings, loaded them into his truck, and taken off.

He was gone.

It hadn't been much of a good-bye. Tobias hadn't even been home. "He doesn't deserve to be able to say good-bye to me," Tobias had said angrily to Nikki. "I don't care when he leaves, just so long as he leaves. I'll see the rest of you tonight." And then he had driven away in his old car, which would become the family car once Mr. Sherman was gone.

Nikki agreed with everything Tobias had said, but she wanted to watch her father drive away. She didn't want any doubt that he had actually left. So she had been standing in the driveway with her mother and Mae when Mr. Sherman tossed his things onto the front seat of the truck and then climbed in after them.

Mrs. Sherman, looking worried but not particularly sad, had said, "And *where* is this job you found?"

Mr. Sherman grunted. "I told you. Alabama."

"You know there's hardly any money in our account. Just enough for a few weeks."

"I'll be sending you money long before then. Quit worrying."

Those had been Mr. Sherman's last words before he'd slammed the door shut, started the engine with a bang, and roared down the lane, his tires sending gravel flying.

Mae, a smile creeping across her face, had turned to Mrs. Sherman and asked, "Can Paw-Paw be our pet now? Can he come in the house?"

Nikki had spotted Paw-Paw, one of the stray dogs she and Mae regularly fed, sitting hesitantly at the edge of their property, and she, too, turned an expectant face to her mother.

"I don't know," said Mrs. Sherman. "What will we do when your father comes back?"

Mae made a pouty face but then said jubilantly to Nikki, "She didn't say no!"

And now it was the next morning, and even though it was a rainy Monday and vacation was over and Mrs. Mandel was gone, Nikki leaped from her bed, whistling "Rudolph the Red-Nosed Reindeer." "Come on, Mae!" she exclaimed as she rummaged through their bureau drawers. "Time to get up. I'll make pancakes for breakfast!"

Later, when the school bus arrived, Nikki ignored the two kids sitting in the front seats who made a great show of holding their noses as she and Mae lurched their way to the rear. She listened to Mae talk about Santa Claus all the way into town.

When at last the bus drew up in front of Camden Falls Elementary, Nikki looked out her window. "There are Olivia and Flora and Ruby," she said, and she ran along the aisle of the bus, pulling Mae behind her.

Nikki and Mae were the last ones to hop down the steps, and they were grinning when they met their friends.

"Dad left yesterday," Nikki announced, but she inclined her head toward Mae as she said this, and Flora and Olivia and Ruby refrained from asking her any questions.

"And Santa Claus is coming soon!" said Mae.

Flora glanced at Olivia and smiled, but her smile

faded when Mae added, "Last year he didn't have a map to our house so he couldn't come."

"Santa needed a map?" Ruby asked.

Mae nodded. "I drew a map and I gave it to Daddy, but Daddy lost it, and Santa couldn't find our house."

Now Flora glanced at Nikki, who mouthed, "I'll tell you later."

"But this year," Mae went on, "I'll give the map to Mommy. She won't lose it. And I'll send my list with the map. I haven't made the list yet, but I'm going to do it soon."

The older girls listened indulgently as Mae chattered on.

"Here's what I'm going to ask Santa for." Mae screwed up her face in concentration. "A doll with clothes. Like party clothes. And a stuffed dog that's as big as Paw-Paw. And a bead kit so I can make necklaces and earrings for Mommy. And a new box of crayons. And a little piano. Oh, and that Twister game. I think I know right and left now," she said, looking dubiously at her hands. "Santa probably can't fit all those things in his pack, but it would be really nice if he could."

The girls had reached Mae's first-grade room, and Nikki shooed her inside. "See you this afternoon," she said.

"Wow," exclaimed Ruby, "Mae sure is excited about Christmas."

"So am I," said Nikki. "Our first Christmas without Dad. The only thing is . . . I hope Mae will be satisfied with just the crayons and maybe the game. There's no way Mom can afford all that other stuff."

"Well," said Flora, "you know what Min would say. 'Let's cross that bridge when we come to it.'"

Nikki nodded.

"Bye, you guys," said Ruby as she opened the door to her fourth-grade room. "I'll see you later."

Nikki, Olivia, and Flora then stood hesitantly outside the door to their own classroom.

"Here goes," said Olivia, sounding as if she were getting ready to jump into a freezing cold swimming pool.

But none of the girls moved.

"It's only Mr. Donaldson," said Flora finally, and although she was the shyest of the three girls, she reached out and opened the door.

"Good morning," said Mr. Donaldson heartily. He was standing behind his desk, wearing a necktie with brilliant goldfish on it.

How bad could a teacher with a fish tie be? thought Nikki. And the day began. It felt, Nikki realized, almost like the first day of school again, and in a way it was, since it was the first day with their new teacher.

"Let's talk about the three hundred and fiftieth birthday celebration," Mr. Donaldson said after he had taken care of all the morning chores, such as attendance and announcements. "Mrs. Mandel told me that there will be a lot of special activities to commemorate Camden Falls's big birthday, and that you're going to be part of them."

Olivia shot her hand in the air, making her pigtails quiver. "Mr. Donaldson," she said, "there are SO many things going on! Our school is putting on a play about the Camden Falls witch trials, and Flora's sister is going to be the star of the play. That's Flora over there," said Olivia, pointing, "and her sister is Ruby. She's in fourth grade. And also, there are going to be all these exhibits in town that anyone can go see, with prizes for the best entries. I'm taking pictures of Camden Falls wildlife for the photography exhibit."

"So," said Mr. Donaldson, "the exhibits are for work by both adults and kids?"

Olivia nodded, wondering why their new teacher didn't know this, and Mary Louise Detwiler said, "Mr. Donaldson, don't you live in Camden Falls?"

"I just moved here," he replied.

Their teacher had a lot to learn. That was clear.

"Well, there are going to be all kinds of exhibits," spoke up Randall Tyler. "Photos, art, history. Plus fun stuff. A parade and a fair."

Flora raised her hand nervously, and when Mr. Donaldson nodded to her, she said, "There's going to be an exhibit of antique clothes and quilts. My grandmother and Olivia's grandmother are organizing that.

They own Needle and Thread, the sewing store. They're going to have a float in the parade, too."

"Will you be helping with the float?" asked Mr. Donaldson.

Flora shook her head. "No. I mean, yes. But I'm — I'm —"

"Mr. Donaldson," said Olivia, "Flora is really shy. She's working on a history project, but she won't talk much about it yet. That's just how she is. She's always private about her works in progress."

"I see," said Mr. Donaldson.

Nikki saw something else. She saw Randall hide a smirk when Olivia mentioned "works in progress," a term that probably only Olivia and Mr. Donaldson understood completely. Nikki wished she were sitting close enough to Randall to give him a good poke in the ribs. Olivia couldn't help being smart any more than Flora could help being shy.

"I have an idea," said Mr. Donaldson. "Why don't we go around the room, and each of you can tell me what you're working on for the celebration. Make sure you say your name first."

One by one, the kids in Nikki's class told Mr. Donaldson their plans. Nikki's heart began to pound. If someone had asked her just the week before what her plans were, she would have replied, "I don't have any." This was because her father had forbidden her to participate in the celebration. "Us Shermans," he had said, "don't need to call any attention to ourselves." (Any *more* attention, Nikki had thought.) But now a wonderful, exciting idea was taking shape in Nikki's mind. Maybe, just maybe, she could enter some of her drawings in the art exhibit. Her father couldn't do anything about that if he was out of town, could he? There was nothing Nikki liked better than drawing (she planned to become a wildlife artist one day), and maybe she could work on some drawings of Camden Falls. Flora and Ruby and Olivia had been encouraging her to enter one of the shows. And now, maybe, she could. Maybe. When had her father said he might come back? In the spring, Nikki remembered. If he bothered to come back at all.

"Next," Mr. Donaldson said, and Nikki realized it was her turn.

She swallowed. "My name is Nikki Sherman," she said, "and I — I might work on some drawings for the art exhibit."

There. She had said it. In front of her teacher and her entire class.

When the last bell of the day rang, Flora grabbed Nikki by the arm and said, "Stay after school with Olivia and me. There's a play rehearsal and I told Ruby we'd come."

"Okay," Nikki replied. "Let me just tell Mae and call my mom."

Later, sitting in the back of the auditorium, only

half listening to Ruby and the others on the stage (Ruby was easy to hear; she had the loudest voice of anyone in the room), Olivia whispered, "Nikki, you have to enter the show! You *have* to. I know your drawings would be the best there."

"It's just that my dad — I don't know when he's going to be back. What if I started working on the drawings and he came home?"

"Well, he wouldn't know what you planned to do with the drawings," Flora pointed out. "Anyway, he won't be back for a while, will he? You could get a head start on them, just in case."

"And if he shows up unexpectedly," added Olivia, "you could move your drawings here to school. Mr. Donaldson wouldn't care. And then if you change your mind about entering, well, it won't matter. But if you don't, you'll be all ready."

"I guess . . ." said Nikki.

"Come on. You know you want to do this," said Flora.

"Besides, what's your father so worried about?" asked Olivia. "If you got a prize, you could show Camden Falls," (Olivia paused, searching for the right words) "you could show Camden Falls the other side of the Shermans."

Nikki grinned. "Okay. I'm going to do it."

"High five!" said Olivia.

CHAPTER 4

A Peek in the Windows

If you were to visit Camden Falls, Massachusetts, in the month of December, you would find a very busy town. Walk down Main Street at the end of the day and you'll see that as darkness gathers and the streetlights blink on, the store windows glow golden. Shoppers are still hurrying along with their packages. In the windows are gingerbread men and chocolate Yule logs, waving Santas, smiling angels, and electric trains winding around miniature villages. There's Mrs. Grindle wearily closing up Stuff 'n' Nonsense after a long day. There's a line of people stretching all the way out the door of the post office, even though closing time is just five minutes away.

Now leave Main Street and walk to Aiken Avenue. The windows of the eight Row Houses glow as cheerfully as the windows in town. If you turn onto Aiken from the direction of Needle and Thread, you'll come first to the house at the left end of the row. That's the Morrises'. They're home from the trip they took over Thanksgiving, and the four Morris kids are already back into their school routine. "And," says Lacey, who's eight, "there are only three weeks until our next vacation. Then it's Christmas!"

Next door to the Morrises, old Mr. and Mrs. Willet are sitting down to supper in the kitchen. Mr. Willet is wondering if he should bother getting a Christmas tree this year. He realizes that his wife won't miss one, and that if they do get one, it might confuse her. But this is to be her last Christmas in the home they have shared for so many years — she'll be moving to Three Oaks in January, to the wing for people with Alzheimer's. How can they have their last Christmas together without a tree? Maybe, he thinks, he'll ask his friends Min Read and Rudy Pennington for their advice.

In the third house, Dr. Malone, the dentist, and his daughters, Margaret and Lydia, have, like the Morrises, returned from their Thanksgiving vacation. Dr. Malone is wondering when he should haul their Christmas decorations out of the attic. Every year he puts together a Christmas for his daughters that he hopes is as lovely as the ones the family shared before his wife died. He wonders, too, if he will always miss his wife as acutely at the holidays as he still does, nearly six years after her death.

Now pass by the next few houses, and walk to the one at the other end of the row. The house here belongs to the Fongs. Their home is buzzing with excitement, and it's all about the baby, as they begin work on the nursery. On this cozy evening, Mr. Fong is seated at a sewing machine, stitching boldly patterned curtains, and Mrs. Fong is painting an underwater mural on one wall of the baby's room.

Next door live the Edwardses, seventeen-year-old Robby and his parents. Tonight Robby is seated at the kitchen table, a pack of crayons and a stack of construction paper before him. "Mom! Mom!" he says. "This year I am going to make all my own cards. Christmas cards and Hanukkah cards. I want to make one for every family here at the Row Houses, and one for every kid in my class. Oh, and for Mrs. Fulton. Can you please write Christmas on one piece of paper and Hanukkah on another piece so I can keep them right here and always know how to spell those long words?" Robby is grinning, and so is his mother as she sets to work making his spelling cards.

To the left of Robby's house is Mr. Pennington's. Mr. Pennington is nearly eighty-three, and he is spending a quiet evening with his old dog, Jacques. This is Mr. Pennington's favorite time of day, that hour just before dinner when the world winds down. He sits on the couch and strokes Jacques's silky ears.

Olivia and her family live on the other side of Mr.

Pennington, and Olivia has always been glad about that. She considers Mr. Pennington her third grandfather. On this evening, Olivia is seated at the desk in her bedroom. She is supposed to be doing her homework, but her mind keeps wandering to Mae Sherman and the map she plans to make for Santa Claus. What will Mae think when she doesn't get the presents she asks Santa for? Every time Olivia imagines Christmas morning at the Shermans', a funny feeling comes over her, an uncomfortable feeling. Olivia brings the cordless phone into her room and dials Flora's number. She presses her ear to the wall; sometimes she can hear the phone ringing on the other side.

Presently, Ruby answers. "Read and Northrop Summer Home," she says. "Some are home, some are not."

Olivia giggles. "Hi, it's me, Olivia. Can you ask Flora to get on the phone, too?"

When Flora has picked up the extension, Olivia says, "I can't stop thinking about Mae and Santa Claus, and I have this idea. Maybe we could surprise Mae with a visit from Santa. If we all worked together, and if we talked to some of the grown-ups, I bet we could get most of the things on Mae's list and then they could be delivered to her by a Santa Claus on Christmas Eve."

Next door, Flora finds this idea so exciting that, after she has hung up the phone, she can no longer concentrate on her homework. So she closes her door and pulls out the secret projects she's working on — presents for Min and Ruby and Olivia and Nikki and all her other new friends, and even Daisy Dear and King Comma.

Flora is wondering what to make for a dog when the phone rings again. This time Min answers it.

"Hi, Mom," says the voice at the other end.

"Allie!" cries Min. "How good to hear from you."

"Did you get my card?"

"Yes, and we're delighted that you'll be coming for Christmas. This will be the girls' first Christmas without their parents, you know, and I wasn't sure about bringing them to New York. I think they'll be happier staying put. But won't you miss Christmas in the city?"

"Not so much," says Allie. "What about you?"

"I guess not so much, either. I've celebrated with you in New York for years, but it will be nice to be here in Camden Falls. Actually, I'm looking forward to it."

"Good."

Allie tells Min that she plans to arrive a few days before Christmas and to stay through New Year's, and Min begins making plans and lists in her head even before she hangs up the phone.

Leave Aiken Avenue now and stroll back to Main Street. Turn a corner at the other end of town, turn another corner, and you'll find yourself on a lane lined with shabby houses. Here's one with two steps leading to the front door, but at the back is a door with no steps at all, and through that window you can see Sonny Sutphin moving around his two-room apartment in his wheelchair. Someone at the little market in the next lane gave him three cans of soup and a package of bologna this afternoon, and Sonny is fixing himself a fine supper of tomato soup and fried bologna.

Leave town behind you now and take a chilly walk along country roads to the Shermans' house. The four people inside are smiling, and look, there's Paw-Paw. Nikki and Mae have fixed a warm shelter for him on the front stoop. Tomorrow he will go to the vet for the first time in his life.

"Paw-Paw must wonder what we're doing," says Nikki. "I bet he's never seen Christmas up close before."

Mrs. Sherman, Tobias, Nikki, and Mae have brought out their box of decorations. They are nothing like the ones that are stored in the attics of most of the Row Houses. What the Shermans have are some paper chains made by Mae in preschool, a wooden angel that Mrs. Sherman has kept since she was a little girl, a Santa doll that's missing its nose, and a pillow with NOEL stitched across the front. There's another box full of ornaments for the tree, but that's all. The Shermans love their decorations, though, and they are pleased with them, so they admire them for a few moments, and then Mae turns her attention to the map and the letter to Santa.

"Letter first," she says, and diligently writes out the list of toys she wants. When she's done, she draws the map, including an enormous arrow pointing to a box with a triangle on top labeled MY HOUS. She gives both pieces of paper to her mother and says, "I know *you* won't lose these."

Mrs. Sherman glances at Tobias, who can't look at either his mother or his little sister. But he doesn't want to ruin the evening, so he says, "Let's think about which tree we're going to cut down this year."

Mae is happy about that, and their preparations continue.

CHAPTER 5

Snow Day

One night just before Ruby climbed into her bed, she stood at the window that looked out over the front yard and thought how very dark Aiken Avenue seemed. At the corner of Dodds Lane a street lamp shone, but there was no moonlight and there were no stars in the sky, either. She raised her window a bit, then shut it quickly.

"*Brr,*" she said aloud. "Too cold for open windows."

She crawled beneath the blankets and a few minutes later felt King Comma leap lightly onto her bed. Ruby held up the covers for him and he slid under and curled into a purring ball behind her knees.

They slept that way the entire night. When Ruby's alarm clock went off the next morning, the first thing she noticed was the odd gray light in her room, seeping around the edges of her window shade. Ruby sat up slowly, then peeked around the shade. She gasped and let the shade fly all the way up.

"Snow!" she cried. "Snow, King Comma! Snow, everybody!"

It was not just a little snow but quite a lot. In the dim light, Ruby could see that the cars on the street had become rounded mounds, like igloos. Snow lay piled against tree trunks. Ruby guessed that the fluffy tower on Mr. Pennington's birdbath, which she could just barely see, was a good foot high. And more snow was falling. It was being flung from the sky, whirling and circling and sometimes appearing to whoosh upward instead of down.

Ruby flew barefoot from her bedroom and into Flora's, not bothering to knock on the door.

"Flora, it's snowing! It's snowing *hard*! I bet we won't have school today."

Flora, whose alarm clock had gone off and who was lying in bed, thinking (and worrying just a little bit about a lot of things), sprang to life. "Really?" she said, hurrying to look out her own window.

"Let's go downstairs and turn on the TV," said Ruby.

"We don't know which channel has the school closings," said Flora.

"Is Min up yet?" Ruby asked as she and Flora ran down the stairs.

Min was up — she was making coffee in the kitchen with Daisy Dear hovering hungrily around her knees.

She didn't know which channel listed the school closings, either.

"Is it too early to call Olivia?" asked Flora.

But just then the phone rang. Ruby grabbed it and heard Olivia's voice on the other end. "It's a huge snowstorm!" she exclaimed. "Almost blizzard conditions! And there's no school today. Turn on channel eight if you want to see for yourselves."

Ruby and Flora made a dash for the television set and turned on channel 8. Running along the bottom of the screen were the names of the schools that would be closed that day. The list was alphabetical and was up to the G's. Flora and Ruby had to wait for it to get all the way around to the C's again. When it did, they clasped hands. A moment later, Ruby let out a whoop. "There it is! There it is! Camden Falls Central Schools — closed!"

"Wa-hoo!" cried Flora, and she and Ruby danced into the kitchen.

"Let's call Nikki," said Ruby. "She must be up by now. Her bus comes early."

"And we don't have to worry that her father will answer the phone," said Flora.

"My land, I've never seen such excitement," said Min a few minutes later when Ruby and Flora finally settled down to breakfast.

"Hey, Min, I have a new expression for you," said Ruby. "It's 'my sainted aunt.' I read it in a book."

Min smiled. "I like that," she said. "Now listen, girls. I have something very important to tell you."

Ruby looked at her grandmother, startled, but Min wore a smile on her face.

"In this house," Min went on, "we have a rule about snow days, especially snow days when you don't have to go to school *and* I don't have to go to Needle and Thread — which I won't have to do until later today. This is the rule: You get to do whatever you want until the snow stops falling. Then you'll come outside and help me shovel our walk. Everyone else will be shoveling, too."

"Whatever we want," Ruby repeated dreamily. There were so many possibilities. Indoor things, outdoor things. She gazed out the window, thinking of snowmen and snow forts.

An unexpected free morning was such a lovely surprise that in the end everyone did more than one thing. Min first read by the fire, then set to work in the sewing room. Flora got out her projects and stitched and glued and cut and stamped until Olivia came over to talk about Mae's Christmas surprise. Ruby rehearsed (loudly) several scenes from the school play, then put on her coat and snow pants and boots and hat and scarf and mittens and went outside to build a snow family with Robby and Olivia's brothers and the Morris kids.

Just after lunchtime, the snow wound down until only a few teeny flakes were falling and Ruby could see patches of blue in the sky.

"Shoveling time," announced Min.

Ruby put all of her outdoor clothes on for the second time, and Min asked her if she would go to the garage and find the snow shovels. "I think they're leaning against the back wall."

By the time Ruby returned with the shovels, most of the Row House neighbors were outside, just as Min had predicted. Olivia and her parents were shoveling their walk, while Henry and Jack, Olivia's brothers, helped Mr. Pennington with his. Robby was working cheerfully alongside his parents, and Dr. Malone was being helped by Margaret and a sullen-looking Lydia. At the south end of the row, Mrs. Morris worked on the walk while Mr. Morris, aided by Lacey and her twin brother, Mathias, began to unbury his car, which unfortunately hadn't been parked in their garage. Ruby looked at the other end of the row and saw the Fongs emerge from their front door, a shovel in Mr. Fong's hand. Only the Willets' walk remained untouched.

The grown-ups called up and down the row, and the children ran from house to house. Mrs. Fong, smiling, revealed a piece of news. "We found out yesterday what the baby is going to be."

"What is it? What is it?" cried Ruby and Lacey.

"A girl."

"Oh, a girl!" said Ruby.

Olivia and Flora let out satisfied sighs. "A girl."

"What are you going to name her?" asked Flora.

"We haven't decided yet."

"We may give her a Chinese name," said Mr. Fong.

"Well, anyway, it's a girl." Ruby had been hoping for a girl. Not that there was anything wrong with boys.

When Min's walk was clear, she said to Ruby and Flora, "All right. I have to go to the store now. Gigi will be there in a few minutes, and we want to open up for the rest of the afternoon. You can stay at the Walters' or the Morrises' — I checked with them — or come to the store later, if you want, okay?"

The thought of seeing Main Street after a snowstorm that was nearly a blizzard was tempting, but Ruby and Flora decided to stay at the Row Houses. Flora went to Olivia's, and Ruby and Lacey were just about to start work on a snow dog when the door to the Willets' house opened and there came Mr. Willet, shovel in hand. Mrs. Willet hovered behind him on the other side of the storm door. Then she stepped tentatively onto the snowy porch in her slippered feet.

"No, dear. You stay inside," said her husband.

Mrs. Willet took another step forward. "My," she said, "this almost reminds me of something."

Mr. Willet returned to the front door. "I have to shovel the walk now. Stay inside, dear. This won't take long."

Mrs. Willet looked confused. She reached for the door handle, then for her husband, and finally bent down and ran her bare hand through the snow.

Next door, Dr. Malone, whose walk was now clear, nudged Lydia. "Why don't you go stay with Mrs. Willet and I'll help Mr. Willet with the shoveling."

Ruby, watching, could tell that Lydia was just dying to make a face or roll her eyes, but she wouldn't, since the Willets were right there. By the time she reached their front stoop, she had put a smile on her face. She removed her boots, stuffed her gloves in her pockets, and took Mrs. Willet by the hand.

"Hi, Mrs. Willet," she said.

"Why, Nancy, it's so nice to see you again," said Mrs. Willet politely. "How lovely of you to drop by."

Lydia looked helplessly over her shoulder at her father, who shook his head slightly. "It's nice to see you, too," Lydia replied.

"Won't you come in for a cup of tea?" asked Mrs. Willet, and she and Lydia disappeared inside.

Mr. Pennington trudged to the Willets' with his snow shovel and lent a hand. "Mary Lou looks well," he said to Mr. Willet.

Mr. Willet nodded. "She does. She has her good days and her bad days. But the good days come less and less often, and the bad days are worse than ever. She's always polite to company, though, even when she doesn't know whom she's talking to." Mr. Willet set his shovel down. "Rudy," he said, "would you come with me one day to visit Three Oaks? I'd like for you to see where Mary Lou will be going."

At this, Ruby thought she noticed a change in Mr. Pennington's face. It was a small change, but a change nevertheless, and when he answered his old friend, Ruby heard just the faintest hardening in his voice. "Certainly," said Mr. Pennington. And then again, "Certainly."

Ruby felt confused but then was distracted by a low humming sound from down the street.

"Snowplow!" cried Jack Walter.

And sure enough, there was a snowplow, making its way slowly along Aiken Avenue.

"That means school tomorrow," said Lacey.

"Oh, well," replied Ruby. "At least we had today."

Ruby sat down on Lacey's front steps and took in the wintry scene — red mittens, striped scarves, snowmen with carrot noses. It all made her think of a Charlie Brown cartoon she had seen on television the year before. And that made her hear Christmas music in her head. And *that* gave her an idea, an idea for a gift she could give her whole family on Christmas morning. It would involve some rehearsing, and she would need to find a book of carols. Ruby figured Ms.

Angelo, who directed the Children's Chorus, must have one.

Ruby sighed with pleasure. A day off from school, an exciting idea, a baby girl on the way — her first snow day in Camden Falls had been more wonderful than she could have hoped.

CHAPTER 6

Olivia's News

Once the cold weather arrived, it stayed. And so the snow stayed, too. Camden Falls became a crunchy, icy town. At night the wind whistled, and during the day the sun, if it came out at all, was weak. Often, more snow fell, but not enough for another snow day.

One blustery evening, Olivia Walter and her family gathered in their kitchen. They were in the midst of a big project, and Olivia felt especially cozy and Christmasy and holidayish.

"It feels like Santa's workshop in here," said Olivia.

"Except that we're not making toys," replied Jack, who was six.

"No, but we're as busy as Santa's elves," said Henry, who was eight.

Olivia looked around the kitchen with a satisfied smile. Her mother was a very creative person, and

Olivia was proud of her. Mrs. Walter liked to cook, but she didn't just cook meals. She baked cookies and brownies and tiny loaves of bread. She made relishes and dips and sauces (butterscotch sauce was Olivia's favorite). And she made candy. Olivia didn't know anyone else, apart from professional candy makers, who made candy. But Mrs. Walter made peanut butter cups and mint patties and chocolate-covered coconut candy and something called chocolate bark. She poured chocolate into molds, too, and made chocolate shells and flowers and birds (for anyone to enjoy), nuts and bolts and saws and hammers (guy treats, she said), bones and paw prints (for animal lovers), and, at this time of year, Santas and bells and wreaths and angels (for Christmas) and menorahs and Stars of David (for Hanukkah). Recently, Mrs. Walter had perfected large chocolate lollipops. Jack's favorites were rubber duckies. Mrs. Walter was so clever that she knew how to mix colors into white chocolate. So the duckies were bright yellow, and Mrs. Walter had shown everyone how to paint the eyes brown or blue and the beaks orange. But for the holidays she was making fir tree lollies and Santa's hat lollies and dreidel lollies. The dreidels were the most difficult (and the most fun) to make, because Mrs. Walter insisted on painting them in so many different colors of chocolate that they looked almost like real dreidels.

And what were the Walters doing with all these

candies and breads and cookies and sauces and lollies? They were putting together holiday gift baskets for their friends. Ordinarily, Mr. and Mrs. Walter would go shopping and buy presents for their friends — carefully chosen presents. But this year neither Mr. nor Mrs. Walter had a job, so they were saving money and having fun at the same time. Mr. Walter, who was as creative as Mrs. Walter (this was one reason he hadn't minded so much when he lost his very boring job with a computer company), had searched the stores on Main Street until he had found a number of pleasing bargains — baskets at half price, a sale on tree ornaments at Bubble Gum, and a bagful of teeny holiday books from Time and Again, the used bookstore. The entire family had driven partway to Somerville to a new dollar store, spent just twenty dollars, and had come away with a giant bagful of ribbon and yarn, dishcloths (Olivia hadn't been sure how these were going to be used), some Christmas fabric, two boxes of candy canes, a bunch of plastic holly, several packages of tiny cellophane baggies, and three rolls of colored cellophane.

And now, despite their budget, the Walters were turning out one fabulous basket after another. No two were alike. Mrs. Walter, the chief cook and candy maker, would set her handiwork on the kitchen table — jars of relish, chocolate sauce, and butterscotch sauce; pans of candy and lollipops; and trays of cookies and breads. Then the fun began. The rest of the Walters were in charge of packaging the food and arranging it in the one-of-a-kind baskets.

"Look," said Henry. "I'm going to put each of the Christmas tree lollipops in a Baggie and tie it with red and white ribbon — the kind you can make into curlicues."

Olivia contemplated the jars and the fabric, then ran to the sewing box for a pair of pinking shears. "I have an idea!" she said. "I'll cut out circles of fabric with the pinking shears, put one on each jar lid, fasten it with yarn, and add a sprig of the holly."

"Both wonderful ideas," said Olivia's mother.

Olivia's father was in charge of assembling the baskets, with help from Jack. And that was when Olivia found out what the dishcloths were for. Her father used them to line the baskets. He shaped each one into a sort of bowl, nestled the jars and the bags of cookies and packages of candy inside, then added a book or an ornament and some candy canes. After that, he and Jack decorated the handle of the basket with ribbons.

"A work of art!" Olivia pronounced when she saw the first finished basket. She went back to covering the jar lids with fabric.

This is the perfect evening, Olivia thought. Her homework was finished, snowflakes were falling gently outside the window, Christmas carols were playing on the radio, and inside the warm kitchen everyone was working happily. Plus, the kitchen smelled of chocolate and cinnamon and ginger and cloves.

And then her father ruined everything, ruined the perfect peaceful evening and all the holiday feelings.

"Kids," he said, "there's something your mother and I want to talk to you about."

"What is it?" said Jack. He was concentrating so hard on wrapping a basket handle with ribbon that his tongue was sticking out of the corner of his mouth.

Mr. Walter sat down in the nearest chair. "As you know, your mother and I have been out of work for a little longer than we thought we would be."

"I thought only *you* were out of work," said Henry.

"Well, your mother has a part-time job now, that's true. But one of us needs to work full-time. And neither of us has found a full-time job that pays enough to support the family."

A funny feeling began to creep around the edges of Olivia's stomach. She didn't know what her father was going to say next, but she was fairly certain she wasn't going to like it.

"So," said Mr. Walter, "your mother and I have been investigating business opportunities a little farther afield."

"What does that mean?" asked Jack.

"It means they've been looking far away," replied Olivia, eyeing her father suspiciously.

"How far away?" said Jack.

"Well, not *too* far away. Somerville, Tillington, Rosedale. An hour or two from Camden Falls."

"We'd really like to find a business we could run together," spoke up Olivia's mother. "Something creative. Like making these gift baskets but on a much larger scale."

"That would be cool," said Jack. "Candy all the time."

"And we've found two commercial spaces for sale," continued Mr. Walter. "One in Somerville and one halfway between Rosedale and Tillington. Neither space is exactly what we're looking for, but both come with professional kitchens and are affordable."

"You would work together all day long?" asked Henry.

"Yes," said Mrs. Walter.

"Then what would *we* do?" Henry wanted to know. "I mean, after school. Would we have baby-sitters?"

Mr. Walter shook his head. "We don't know. We haven't planned that far ahead. What we have thought about, though, is the fact that we don't want to live quite so far from where we work. So we would probably —"

"Don't say it!" Olivia cried suddenly. "Really. Don't say it."

"Move," said her father. "I'm sorry, Olivia, but that's what we've been thinking about. And we want you to be prepared for the possibility."

"But I can't move!" said Olivia. "I can't leave here. Camden Falls, the Row Houses. I grew up here. *You* grew up here, Mom. In this house. How could you leave it? How could you leave Camden Falls? I don't want to live anywhere else."

"Me, neither," said Jack and Henry in one voice, but not nearly as vehemently as Olivia, and then Henry said, "Hey! We're almost out of red ribbon."

"Henry, how on earth can you think of red ribbon at a time like this?" exclaimed Olivia, who really felt a little like she might cry. She didn't want her brothers to know this, though, so she added, "Stupid idiot."

"Olivia," said Mr. Walter warningly.

"Well, he is. And anyway, it's entirely unfair of you to ask *us* to move. We're not the ones who lost our jobs."

This time it was Mrs. Walter who exclaimed "Olivia!" only she sounded both shocked and angry. She removed a pot of melted chocolate from the stove, set it on a trivet, and turned to face her daughter. "Please apologize to your father," she said.

"Sorry," said Olivia, and she felt tears gather in her eyes. She set down the pinking shears and plopped onto a chair.

"Honey." Mr. Walter stood up and put his arm around Olivia.

Olivia squirmed away from him. "I can't leave my friends," she cried, and then the tears slid down her cheeks. "*All* my friends are here. And my school and

Needle and Thread and Gigi and Poppy. How can you ask me to leave everything?"

"We know it wouldn't be easy," said Mrs. Walter. "We know you don't want to move —"

"Then don't make me," said Olivia.

"But this is very important," continued her mother.

"We can't be out of work for too much longer," added her father. "And we very much want a business we can run together. I wasn't happy at the company, and your mother would like to put her many talents to work."

"But — but my room," said Olivia desperately. "I've never had another bedroom. I don't want another bedroom. And I don't want new friends or to go to a new school and be the new kid in class."

"Well," said Mr. Walter finally, "it might not happen. We haven't decided to buy either of the places we found. We're still looking. We just wanted you to know it was a possibility. We didn't want to take you by surprise one day and announce that we really are moving."

"This is just as bad," said Olivia. "Now I won't be able to do anything but worry until you make up your minds."

"I'm not worrying," said Henry.

"Me, neither," said Jack. "Moving would be cool. I like moving vans."

Olivia refrained from saying that the moving van would only be around for a day or two and then they would be stuck for years and years in some strange town with no friends until they were old enough to move back to Camden Falls where they belonged, and when they did, there probably wouldn't be a Row House available to move into anyway.

Olivia slumped in her chair. "Christmas is ruined," she said. "Everything is ruined."

Henry looked up from his lollipop packages, which he was now tying with green and white ribbon. "You know what you are, Olivia?" he said. "A drama queen."

"I am not a drama queen!" cried Olivia. "But you know who is? Ruby. And you know who I will never, ever get to see again after we move? Ruby."

"Honey, that's not true," said Mrs. Walter. "We're only talking about moving an hour or so away. You could visit with Ruby and Flora and Nikki and anyone else easily. We'd just have to do a little more driving."

"It wouldn't be the same."

"No. That's true. It wouldn't be exactly the same. But it wouldn't mean losing your friends, either."

"I don't care. I want things exactly the same."

"I'm afraid, Olivia, that things never stay *exactly* the same. They change all the time. Children grow up and towns grow bigger and people come and go."

"Well, I don't like any of those things," declared Olivia. "I didn't want Mrs. Mandel to move away or Mr. Donaldson to come."

"What if," said Mrs. Walter, "Flora and Ruby hadn't moved here? Would you like that?"

"No," mumbled Olivia. "But I still don't want to move. And you can't *make* me want to move." Olivia rose and looked around at each member of her family. "I will *never* want to move," she added fiercely, and then she fled to her room, her old familiar room, where she patted her guinea pig and stared out her window at the snow.

CHAPTER 7

Buttons and Beads

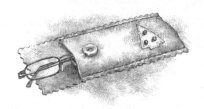

"Mmm, it smells divine in here," said Ruby dramatically. She surveyed Needle and Thread, which was all ready for the first of its gift-making events. Min and Gigi had arrived at the store earlier than usual that morning and made two pots of coffee and a pot of tea. The table at the front of the store, which was usually covered with sewing magazines, had been cleared for the plates of cookies and muffins and sticky buns that Needle and Thread customers would bring by.

"Everything *looks* divine, too," said Flora, eyeing the back of the store where several worktables were now lined up, surrounded by chairs that Min and Gigi had borrowed from Camden Falls Elementary. Piled on one end of each table were all sorts of supplies: fleece and satin and felt, precut patchwork pieces, buttons, beads, laces, embroidery ribbon and thread, and scissors and needles and rulers and pins and fabric markers. Stacked next to the supplies were sheets of instructions for making pillows and eyeglass cases and sachets and tote bags and fleece scarves.

"Of course," said Gigi, "people can make anything they want. They don't have to stick to these projects. We just thought the directions might be helpful."

"How many people do you think will come today?" asked Ruby. There was nothing she liked better than a good turnout.

"We're not sure," replied Gigi. "A lot of people said they wanted to help, but we're having two events, so some people will come next week."

Ruby eyed the clock. "It's still early," she said.

Two hours later, the store was bustling.

Nikki and Olivia had arrived, and Min had put them, along with Ruby and Flora, in charge of walking around the tables, answering questions, summoning Min or Gigi when necessary, and helping kids who were having trouble. Nearly every seat at the tables was filled, and more people were sitting on the couches by the front door as well, all stitching away happily.

From time to time, Olivia would step away from all the activity, sit quietly, look around the store, and wonder how many more times she would see this particular scene — the familiar store, these people she loved. Olivia felt that she could disappear from it in a flash.

Ruby, however, smiled as she watched Dr. Malone

select a piece of red-and-white fleece and set to work on a scarf. She looked happily at Robby, who had arrived early and had been working all morning on a tote bag. And she watched with amusement as Flora continually eyed the stack of directions for making lavender-scented sachets. Flora had written the directions herself and was very proud of them.

"Hi, Mr. Pennington!" said Flora cheerfully when he entered the store. "Are you here to make gifts?"

"I certainly am. Put me to work."

"Wouldn't you like some refreshments first?" asked Ruby.

"Thank you, but not quite yet. I'll save the refreshments for later, when I need a break."

Ruby ushered Mr. Pennington to the back of the store and pulled out a chair that had just been vacated. "Why don't you sit here? You can make anything you want —"

"But the sachets are very nice," interrupted Flora. "Would you like to make a sachet? It would be the perfect gift for someone. See, you fill it with dried lavender flowers — they have a wonderful scent — and flax seeds to give it a little weight. The sachets look very fancy, but you can make one in just a couple of hours."

"Well, I —" said Mr. Pennington.

"Here, I'll help you get started," said Flora. "Now, the idea is to choose some of the more lush fabrics, like these satins. You piece together a square that's not bigger than about seven inches, and you decorate it with lace and buttons. These buttons are nice; they look like antiques. You put the buttons on *before* you sew the front to the back because otherwise you have to reach through your opening for turning, and that's too small. Oh — a lot of people have been putting piping around the edges of the pillow before they attach the backing. I don't know how much sewing you've done —"

"Flora?" said Min, approaching the tables. "Are you sure Mr. Pennington wants to make a sachet? Did you show him all the other projects and mention that actually he can make anything at all?"

Mr. Pennington looked at Min with a half smile on his face. Then he turned to Flora. "You know, I'm afraid I'm not quite handy enough to make one of the sachets, although they are lovely. I thought I might try a scarf."

"I'll help you get started," said Min.

Flora, disappointed, retreated to the front of the store for a sticky bun.

At lunchtime, Robby left, handing Ruby a handsome striped tote bag.

"Thank you," said Ruby. "Someone will be very happy to get this."

Robby smiled. "Here. I made this, too. You can put it with the bag." He gave Ruby a small card. On it he had written *Happy Holidays! Made for you by Robby.*

"Hey! That's a great idea!" said Ruby. "Everyone

should do that. The gifts will be more personal if they come with cards."

The store grew quiet at lunchtime, then busy again in the afternoon. Ruby ran around so much that her feet began to hurt.

She called for Gigi when Margaret Malone needed help with her eyeglass case. "I can't remember how to make a French knot," said Margaret, sounding frustrated.

She tried to be patient with a very fussy man who complained that the directions for the projects weren't clear enough.

She ran for Min when a woman seated at a sewing machine broke a needle, causing the machine to stick.

And she gave Jack Walter a hug when he handed her the paper wreath he had made. "I can't sew too good yet," he whispered to her.

By four o'clock the finished gifts were stacked at the checkout counter in several teetering piles that reminded Ruby of the cover of *Caps for Sale*, a book she had asked her parents to read over and over to her when she was small.

"Look at everything!" she exclaimed. And she and Flora and Nikki and Olivia eyed the stacks with as much pride as if they had made all the gifts themselves.

"Mary embroidered those," said Flora, pointing to a pair of ivory pillowcases embellished with delicate roses. "All the roses are bullion knots."

Nikki was busy counting things. "Six tote bags," she announced, "four eyeglass cases, nine pillows . . . Hey, who made that?"

It was a knitted sweater. "Gigi," said Olivia. "She's been working on it for weeks." Olivia paused. She longed to tell her friends about her parents' stunning news. She could actually feel a heaviness in her chest. But every time she thought about speaking the words, something held them back, and they remained locked in Olivia's heart.

"You know what?" said Nikki. "We should have a present-wrapping day next."

"Oh, that's a good idea," said Ruby, and then the bell over the door jangled and Ruby looked up to see Mrs. Grindle enter Needle and Thread.

Olivia narrowed her eyes. "What's the Grinch doing here?" she whispered. She glanced at Nikki, who was inching her way toward the back of the store.

Mrs. Grindle heaved herself down onto one of the couches, emitting a great sigh as she did so.

"Land sakes," said Min. "Is everything all right, Gina?"

"I'm just pooped, that's all. Thank goodness for your mother, Olivia," Mrs. Grindle added. "She's across the street closing up the store. A bit early — what a busy day we had."

"Isn't that a good thing?" asked Ruby, who had

vowed never to speak to Mrs. Grindle again if she could possibly help it. But now she forgot the promise, because what Mrs. Grindle had just said didn't make any sense. "Don't you want lots of business? We do, at Needle and Thread."

"Yes, of course," said Mrs. Grindle. "But, well, I suppose I'm just getting older. A day like today is too much for me now. I'm not the only one who feels this way, though. Ellen and Carol said Ma Grand-mère seems more like a burden than a pleasure these days." Mrs. Grindle kicked off her shoes (the sight of her crooked toes causing Ruby, Olivia, and Flora to suppress giggles) and said, "My feet never used to hurt this much."

"Have some tea," said Min.

"Thank you," replied Mrs. Grindle. She was silent for a moment, then said, "I opened Stuff 'n' Nonsense nearly thirty years ago. That's hard to believe. I used to look forward to the busy times, like the holidays. This year I dreaded it."

"Perhaps you need more help in the store," suggested Gigi.

"You could hire my mother full-time," said Olivia, feeling hopeful. Maybe a full-time job would keep her parents in Camden Falls.

"Or what about shorter hours?" said Min. "You could open at eleven every morning, instead of nine. Or close the store an extra day each week."

Mrs. Grindle stared out the window at Stuff 'n' Nonsense. "I don't know. I really am very tired, and all your suggestions are good ones. But, well, I dislike change."

Huh, thought Olivia. She never dreamed she had anything in common with the Grinch.

CHAPTER 8

Sheltering Arms

Nikki couldn't remember if her father had said when he would be in touch with the Shermans. She didn't think he had given them an actual date. He hadn't, for instance, said, "I'll call you on the fifth." But as December wore on, she was more and more surprised not to have heard from him. For one thing, with cell phones and computers and overnight mail, it was hard *not* to be in touch in some fashion. True, the Shermans didn't have a computer or any cell phones. But they had a regular telephone, and there was nothing wrong with their mail delivery.

Even so, they hadn't heard a word from Mr. Sherman.

"Are you surprised?" Tobias asked Nikki when she mentioned this to him one evening.

"No. I'm not sad, either. But I'm beginning to get a little worried."

"About what?"

Nikki and Tobias were talking quietly in the living room, Paw-Paw at their feet, while their mother put Mae to bed.

"I don't know," replied Nikki. "Worried that something happened to him. Or that he doesn't really plan to come back."

"Would either thing be such a tragedy?" asked Tobias.

Nikki looked at her brother in confusion. "I don't want anything to *happen* to him," she insisted. "I don't want him to get hurt."

"He never loved us," said Tobias.

"I know, but I still don't . . ." Nikki didn't finish her thought. Sometimes there was no point in arguing with Tobias. Finally, she said, "Plus . . . well, we need the money he said he would send us."

"Now *that's* something to worry about," Tobias agreed.

Mrs. Sherman tiptoed into the living room then. "Mae's finally asleep," she said. "Honestly, the closer it gets to Christmas, the harder it is for her to fall asleep."

Nikki nodded. "Because of Santa," she said. Then, "Mom?"

"Yes?"

"Dad hasn't sent you any money yet, has he?"

"No."

"I didn't think so. I mean, I figured you'd tell us if you heard from him." She paused, scratching Paw-Paw's ears. "So what are we going to do?"

"How about celebrate?" suggested Tobias.

"I'm serious," said Nikki. "We need money."

"There's the welfare office . . ." said Mrs. Sherman reluctantly.

"That's not going to cover all the stuff on Mae's Christmas list," said Nikki. Silence. "She can't be disappointed again," she added.

"I love her, but she asked for too much," said Tobias. "Still . . . maybe I could get another after-school job."

"No," their mother said firmly. "One job is enough for you. You need to keep up with your schoolwork. I'm looking for a job myself. A full-time job. It's going to take some time, though. I have to find something that will pay enough to support the entire family. I mean, if we don't hear from your father soon."

Nikki sighed. So many ifs and uncertainties. She knew that Mrs. DuVane, who had helped out her family for years, could probably lend a hand, but even that might not be enough.

"No matter what, Christmas will be more peaceful this year," said Tobias.

Nikki nodded grimly.

"Come on," Tobias continued. "Let's think of

something wonderful to do for Mae, something that doesn't cost any money. Or much money. Like build her a playhouse. We have plenty of lumber and scraps."

"That's great, but she has her heart set on a visit from Santa." Nikki was going to remind Tobias and her mother about last year's disappointment when she saw tears in her mother's eyes. "Never mind," she said. "We can get her a lot of inexpensive stuff. We don't have to get what's on the list. She probably won't care. As long as she thinks Santa brought it."

Nikki went to bed that night feeling guilty. She hadn't wanted to upset her mother. And Tobias had had a good idea. There was probably something wonderful that he and Nikki could do for Mae. They just needed to be a little creative.

In school the next day, Nikki's mind wandered. She thought of her messy yard, the yard that was littered with lumber and old cars and unfinished projects her father had started. What could she and Tobias make for Mae? A playhouse? A dollhouse? Maybe a chest for her toys? Tobias could build the chest and Nikki could paint it. That was a possibility. And they could put it under the tree as if it were a gift from Santa.

When the bus — the smelly, jouncing, crowded bus that was the bane of Nikki's existence — had dropped her and Mae at the end of their lane that afternoon, Nikki discovered that they were the only ones at home. Tobias was still at school, and her mother was at the grocery store (according to the note Nikki found on the kitchen table). Nikki dropped her books in her bedroom, then she and Mae ran outside to the shed where Nikki kept the food for the stray dogs that hung about the edges of their yard. When Mr. Sherman had been around, the dogs had kept their distance and Nikki had been forced to feed them in secret, which meant they weren't fed regularly. Now Nikki fed them like clockwork (she spent almost all of her pocket money on their food), and the dogs were looking fatter.

Also, there were more of them.

"Where are you guys *coming* from?" Nikki asked. She tried not to sound worried or irritated — after all, the dogs depended on her. But still . . .

Nikki had just filled the last bowl when she heard her brother's car on the drive. Five minutes later, Tobias was at her side.

"Geez, how many *are* there?" he asked, looking at the nervous dogs clustered around the dishes.

"More than before," Nikki answered uncomfortably. "But never mind. You know what, Tobias?" Nikki glanced across the yard at Mae, who was sitting on the porch with Paw-Paw. "I was thinking. I like your idea about building something for Mae. We could make it really special."

"Nikki, seriously, you kind of have a problem with the dogs here."

"I know."

"You have to do something."

"You're as bad as Dad!" Nikki exclaimed.

Tobias made a face at her. "I am not," he said mildly, "and you know it."

"Yeah. But . . . I don't know what to do. I can't just stop feeding the dogs. That would be cruel."

"I think you should talk to the people at the animal shelter."

"The animal shelter?! No way. You know what they do to animals there."

"They find homes for them."

"They *try* to find homes for them. But if they can't do it fast enough, they put them to sleep." She paused. "They *kill* them."

"Not every shelter does that. And the new one, the one that was just built — it's called Sheltering Arms — is supposed to be a very good place. I think we should go there and talk to someone."

This was how, two days later, Nikki found herself sitting next to her brother in the Shermans' old car, Tobias at the wheel, Flora in the backseat.

Flora was there for moral support. "Please, please come with me to the shelter this afternoon," Nikki had begged her at school. She had begged Olivia and Ruby, too, but they couldn't come.

Flora was free, though, and got permission from

Min to ride to Sheltering Arms with Nikki and Tobias. "Just promise me you won't come back with any more pets," Min had said. "Daisy Dear and King Comma are quite enough."

Now Tobias was driving slowly along a road Nikki hadn't been on before. It wound through hills and fields outside of Camden Falls, everything lightly covered with a fresh snowfall. "I think it's right around here somewhere," he said. "I've passed it a couple of times."

"Oh! There's the sign," said Flora. "'Sheltering Arms,'" she read. "'A safe haven for stray, abandoned, and abused animals.'"

"See?" said Tobias. "That doesn't sound like the name of a place where animals are put to sleep, does it?"

"No," admitted Nikki. Still, she reached over her seat and clasped Flora's hand.

The woman seated at the front desk of Sheltering Arms was young and friendly — not at all like an animal killer. "May I help you?" she said when Nikki, Flora, and Tobias stepped through the door.

Tobias took charge. "This is my sister Nikki," he said. "We live out in the country." He told the woman about the stray dogs and explained that their numbers were increasing. "And so I think we need to do something," he said finally.

"But I love the dogs!" Nikki blurted out. "I want to help them. And I don't want you to kill any of them!"

"I can assure you," the woman said seriously, "that we do not kill animals here. Not unless they are very ill or have been seriously injured and are in pain and won't be able to recover."

"But I can't bear to think of them in cages, either," said Nikki, who felt dangerously close to tears.

The woman held up her hand. "That's why I think Sheltering Arms is the perfect place for them," she said. "I'd like for you to talk with Ms. Hewitt now. She's our expert on stray dogs."

With that, Nikki, Flora, and Tobias were ushered into a small office where a very nice woman brought in extra chairs so they could all sit down, offered them bottles of water, thanked them for being responsible citizens, and generally treated them like adults.

"What we'll do," Ms. Hewitt explained, "is come to your property from time to time and humanely trap the dogs. *Humanely*," she repeated when she saw the look on Nikki's face. "Then we'll transport the dogs back here, give them vaccinations and rabies shots, treat any wounds or illnesses we detect, and spay or neuter each one. Do you know why spaying and neu-tering is important?"

"So they can't keep on having puppies?" asked Flora.

"Exactly," said Ms. Hewitt. "Each animal we spay or neuter prevents thousands of other strays from being born. After the dogs have recovered," she went on, "we'll keep them here while we try to find homes for them. You can see that we have very few cages at Sheltering Arms. The ones we do have are for dogs who are ill or recovering from surgery. Otherwise, our dogs can play in those large outdoor areas." (Ms. Hewitt gestured at the window, through which Nikki could see a group of dogs playing with toys in an enormous outdoor enclosure.) "Or come inside to our 'living rooms.' I'll show you the living rooms later. They're rooms — *not* cages — with actual furniture in them so that stray dogs can get used to a home environment before they're adopted."

"And what about the dogs who aren't adoptable?" asked Tobias.

"They're welcome to stay here for the rest of their lives."

"And they're never put in cages?" asked Nikki.

"Not unless they're ill and need to be watched closely."

Nikki looked joyously from Flora to her brother to Ms. Hewitt. "This sounds like a dream," she said. "A good dream. I know more dogs will probably show up at home, and I like feeding them. But I need help. And I want the dogs to find homes."

"You can call on us anytime," said Ms. Hewitt. "We'll be sending someone to your property in the next couple of days, as soon as we talk to your mother."

Nikki left Sheltering Arms thinking that the dogs were going to get an unexpected Christmas present.

CHAPTER 9

Three Oaks

"I've never been to an old people's home before," Ruby whispered to Flora.

"Yes, you have. You just don't remember," Flora whispered back. "And don't say 'old people's home.' It's an assisted living community. Mr. Willet said so."

"When was I at an, um, assisted thing?" asked Ruby.

"When you were four and we were visiting Dad's aunt. I'll tell you more about it later. We have to stop whispering. It isn't polite."

It was a Saturday morning and Flora, Ruby, Min, Mr. Pennington, and Mr. Willet were crowded into the Willets' car on their way to visit Three Oaks, where Mrs. Willet would soon be moving. (Min had taken the morning off from the store.) Mr. Willet was at the wheel, Mr. Pennington beside him, and Flora, Ruby, and Min sat in the back. Ruby was in the middle because her legs were the shortest and she would be the least bothered by putting her feet up on the hump. That was what Flora had said, anyway, and now Ruby was attempting to prove her wrong by letting her legs slide off the hump and bump Flora's ankles. Flora wanted to kick her sister, but even more so, she wanted Mr. Willet and Mr. Pennington to see how completely grown up she was, so she moved her legs delicately to the side and looked primly out the window.

"Here we are," said Mr. Willet a few minutes later. He approached a stoplight, where he turned left onto a long drive.

Flora could see a cluster of low buildings.

"Those are apartments for independent living," said Mr. Willet, as though he could read Flora's mind. "They're really lovely. They come in various sizes — one bedroom, two bedrooms. And each one has either a patio with a garden or an upstairs terrace. But Mary Lou will be moving to the facility for people with Alzheimer's, people who are having problems with their memory and with caring for themselves." Mr. Willet turned right and drove around the apartments.

Flora saw a sign that read D-WING PARKING, and Mr. Willet pulled into the lot.

Everyone climbed out of the car. Flora looked at the building that stretched in front of her. Privately, she thought it rather dreary. The stucco sides were painted a very pale yellow. Evenly spaced from one end of the building to the other was a row of wood-framed windows. The windows didn't have shutters, and to Flora they looked like eyes without lashes. She could see a few bare trees and noticed that hanging from two of them were bird feeders. Even so, she found D-Wing a bleak place.

"It's not very cheerful, is it?" Ruby whispered, and Flora nudged her. Would Ruby never figure out when to keep her mouth closed?

"I know it doesn't look like much from out here," said Mr. Willet, and Flora glared at her sister, desperately hoping that Mr. Willet hadn't heard what she'd said. "But it's really a nice place. Wait until we're inside."

"Has Mrs. Willet been here?" asked Flora. "Does she know she'll be moving here?"

"She's visited several times," Mr. Willet replied. "She came here to be evaluated and to meet with the staff and for a tour. But I don't think she remembers the visits, and she doesn't realize that she'll be leaving the Row Houses."

Flora wanted to ask Mr. Willet about a hundred more questions (among them, "Will Mrs. Willet be sad to leave the Row Houses?" and "What if she doesn't want to stay once she gets here?"), but she knew better than to ask them now.

They reached the door to the dreary building, and Mr. Willet opened his wallet, consulted a piece of paper, put the wallet back, then punched a code into a keypad by the door.

"Good security," said Min.

Mr. Willet nodded. "You have to enter the same code when you leave, but that's so the residents can't wander off by themselves," he said sadly.

"You mean Mrs. Willet will be locked in here?" exclaimed Ruby.

"I know it seems cruel," said Mr. Willet, "but she'll be much safer that way. If she left this building she wouldn't know where she was, and worse, she wouldn't know how to ask for help or be able to tell anyone where she lives."

Mr. Willet held the door open and Flora was the first to step through it. She found herself in a wide hallway with a red rug and several brightly colored armchairs. The walls were covered with finger paintings, each paper carefully labeled: *Jamie S., 5 years; Taisha, 4 years.*

"Those were done by the children at the day care center," said Mr. Willet. "The day care center is for kids whose parents work here. Sometimes the children visit with the residents or put on plays or holiday programs for them. And some of the residents — not in this building, but the ones who live in the apartments — volunteer at the center."

Flora began to feel more cheerful.

Mr. Willet approached a desk, a gently curving

polished wood desk on which were arranged a vase of flowers, a small stuffed bunny, a plaque reading HANG IN THERE — IT'S ALMOST FRIDAY, a tiny decorated Christmas tree, and a bowl of foil-covered chocolates. On the wall behind the desk was a calendar featuring a picture of a menorah. Next to that a large sign proclaimed, TODAY IS SATURDAY, DECEMBER 15TH. THE WEATHER IS CLOUDY AND COLD.

"That sign is for the residents," Mr. Willet told Flora and Ruby. "It's easy for them to lose track of things. The information helps to . . ." He paused, thinking.

"To orient them?" suggested Flora.

"Yes!" said Mr. Willet. "Exactly."

"Hello, Mr. Willet," said a cheerful-looking man seated behind the desk. "How have you been?"

"Very well, thank you. Mr. Anderson, these are my friends. This is Mindy Read, Rudy Pennington, and Flora and Ruby Northrop. I was wondering if I could give them a quick tour. I'd like for them to see where Mary Lou will be living."

"Certainly," said Mr. Anderson. "You know your way around. You came on a good day. Everyone is decorating the Christmas tree in the activities room."

Mr. Willet turned to his friends. "In that case, I'll show you some of the residents' rooms first. Most of them will be empty, so we won't disturb anyone."

Flora and the others followed Mr. Willet down a

hall. It was hung with paintings and photographs, pictures of people and animals and foreign cities.

Mr. Willet pointed to a painting of a street in London. "That's Mrs. Willet's favorite picture. She says so every time we visit. I don't know why she likes it so much — she can't explain — but she always pauses to study it. Now, here," he continued, "are the rooms. I suppose it's all right to poke our heads into a couple of them."

Flora peered into the rooms with interest. They weren't big, but each looked more like a cozy bedroom than a hospital room. Still, she wasn't sure she would want to move here and tried to imagine Mrs. Willet as she left the big Row House for this small room.

"We can bring as much of our own furniture as we want," said Mr. Willet. "Except for the bed. Mary Lou will have to use the Three Oaks hospital bed. But we'll be bringing her bureau, a couple of armchairs and tables, and, of course, lots of smaller personal items — pillows and photos and knickknacks and so forth. Oh, hello! Look here, everyone. This is Panda." Mr. Willet stooped to pick up a large black-and-white cat. "Panda and his sister Honey live here. They have the run of the place."

"Hi, Panda," said Flora and Ruby. They stroked his head, and when Mr. Willet set him down, he came along for the rest of the tour. Panda, Flora thought, must be a great comfort to the people who lived here. She pictured him curled up on the end of Mrs. Willet's bed.

Mr. Willet showed them a beauty parlor and barbershop, a small gift shop, a fitness room full of exercise equipment, and a dining room. The dining room, Flora thought (and hoped Ruby wouldn't say out loud), looked as dreary as the outside of the building, but she found the rest of the building quite pleasant and was pleased when everyone they met smiled and greeted Mr. Willet by name.

"Now," said Mr. Willet at last, "here's the activities room."

Flora peered into a large, brightly lit room with lots of tall windows that looked out onto a snowy hillside. Christmas music was playing loudly, and in a corner of the room stood an artificial tree, haphazardly hung with paper snowflakes (which Flora thought had probably been made by the children in the day care center) and colored balls. A woman wearing a red-and-green smock had taken an old man by the hand and was guiding him to the tree. "Put that ornament wherever you like," she said, handing him a snowflake.

The old man was the only one decorating the tree. Eleven other residents were in the room, but six of them were in wheelchairs that had been arranged in a semicircle, and four of those people appeared to be asleep, heads tipped back, mouths open. Flora was shocked to see that one man had not a single tooth in his mouth. The other residents wandered around the room. Two women were mumbling to themselves, and another was humming under her breath. A man dressed in a three-piece suit was standing by the windows, saying loudly, "I told you I haven't had my dinner yet. I want my dinner!"

Flora glanced at Mr. Pennington and thought she saw tears in his eyes. She inched closer to him and took his hand. Mr. Pennington managed a wavering smile.

"This is a good place for Mrs. Willet, isn't it?" Flora said to him. "It's a little sad, but it's nice, too. Everyone smiles, and they think up nice things, like having Panda and Honey around. And it's good to have activities, even when people can't really *do* the activities. I mean, it's always nice to be included. Mrs. Willet will be safe, and there's more for her to do here than there is at home. And Mr. Willet can visit her whenever he wants."

Flora felt pleased when she saw Mr. Pennington brighten a bit. "You know what?" she added as they turned to leave. "I might come here sometimes with Mr. Willet, if it's all right. I might like to help out here." And they walked outside, Min smiling, Mr. Pennington trying to smile, and Mr. Willet saying, "I do think it's the right place for Mary Lou."

CHAPTER 10

Wassail, Wassail!

Open House in Camden Falls was one of Olivia's favorite events of the year. She liked it as much as trick-or-treating on Main Street and the Memorial Day parade, in which once, dressed as a petunia, she had ridden on a float. On the night of Open House, all the stores in town stayed open late and served snacks and hot cider and coffee, and people bundled up to do their last-minute holiday shopping. Groups of carolers wove through the crowds singing Christmas songs, and everyone felt festive and merry.

Olivia's family walked into town at just the hour when, on an ordinary day, Needle and Thread would be closing. In Olivia's pocket was a piece of paper on which she had written her Christmas shopping list. Her parents didn't need to do much shopping (their baskets were coming along nicely), but they said they couldn't miss the annual event. "I'm glad I don't have to work tonight," added Mrs. Walter.

As they walked down Aiken Avenue, their breath forming misty puffs, the scent of pine needles and wood smoke in the frosty air, Olivia thought of Open House the year before. Flora and Ruby hadn't lived next door then, and Olivia hadn't known Nikki well or had any close friends, but how happy she had been that night. Her father still had his job at the computer company, and the thought, the horrible thought, of living some-where other than Camden Falls had never entered Olivia's mind.

Now it was almost all she could think about. And still she hadn't mentioned it to Nikki or Ruby or Flora. She couldn't. For one thing, she didn't think she could bear to see the stunned looks which, she was certain, would cross the faces of her friends. For another, Olivia felt that if she talked about the possibility of moving, she would somehow make it actually happen.

So Olivia walked silently into town with a heavy heart, wondering if she would ever again enjoy life.

"We have to remember to look for Ruby and Lacey," said Henry suddenly. "They get to wear costumes. Old-fashioned costumes."

The carolers this year were members of the Camden Falls Children's Chorus, and they were going to dress as children from nineteenth-century London.

"I get to wear a long coat and a velvet bonnet,"

Ruby had said, "and carry a fur muff. Fake fur," she had added hastily, knowing how Olivia felt about killing animals for their fur. "And on my feet, those little boot things with lots of buttons. They take a long time to fasten."

The Walters turned onto Main Street and, despite her gloomy mood, Olivia brightened when she saw the twinkling stores and the crowds of people, smelled a heady mixture of cinnamon and apples and coffee and peppermint, and heard the high, clear voices of the Children's Chorus.

"Wassail, wassail, all over the town! Our toast it is white and our ale it is brown . . ."

"Just like carolers in old London probably sang," said Henry, who had watched *A Christmas Carol* on television the night before.

Other lilting voices drifted across the street. *"Please bring us some figgy pudding, please bring it right here!"*

"I wonder which group Ruby and Lacey are with," said Olivia, standing on tiptoe and craning her neck.

"Olivia!" someone called then, and Olivia turned to find Nikki hurrying toward her.

"You came!" said Olivia.

Nikki grinned. "Tobias drove me. He's going to pick me up later. Where's Flora?"

"At the store, I think. Mom, Dad, can Nikki and Flora and I go shopping by ourselves? We promise to check in with Gigi every half hour."

Permission was granted, and Olivia and Nikki ran to Needle and Thread.

"It's your first Open House, Flora," said Olivia.

"Mine, too," said Nikki.

And laughing, feeling excitement swell up inside them, they left the store and joined the crowds on Main Street.

"Now — I have a shopping list," said Olivia, sounding official.

"Me, too," said Flora.

"I have a list in my head," said Nikki. "But I don't have much money, so I have to be very careful."

None of them had much money as it turned out. But it didn't matter. Shopping could always be finished another day. The fun of Open House was greeting friends, and looking for Ruby and Lacey, and seeing what treats each store was offering.

"You won't need to eat dinner tonight," Olivia said confidently to her friends. "Let's go to Ma Grand-mère first. Last year they had cookies and gingerbread."

And so the evening began. The girls ate cookies at Ma Grand-mère (which, Olivia thought, would be the perfect store for her parents to buy, what with the professional kitchen and all), sampled candy at Time and Again, and more candy at the hardware store, then drank hot chocolate at Frank's Beans. At each store they consulted their lists (Nikki ran through her mental list) and looked for specials.

"I want to get some Playmobil stuff for Jack," said Olivia, "but only if I can find it on sale."

"I want to get some toys for Mae," said Nikki, "but, unfortunately, I can only afford two of the things on her list for Santa." (At this, Olivia and Flora exchanged smiles.) "Twister and the crayons. And maybe I could get some plastic barrettes or scrunchies for her hair. What I've been thinking is that *we* all know what's on her list, but *she* hasn't seen it since she gave it to Mom, so maybe she's forgotten exactly what she asked for." Nikki looked dubious. "I have this funny feeling, though, that she memorized the list."

The girls came to the window of Bubble Gum and Flora said, "Oh, look! Pens. I want to find a special one for my aunt. She's a writer, you know, so that should be a good gift for her. Hey, and they're on sale."

"And there's a tiara that only costs two dollars and thirty-nine cents," said Nikki. "Mae would like a tiara. I could get that instead of barrettes. She could play princess."

The girls went inside, helped themselves to a tray of gingerbread men, and then Flora chose a beaded pen for her aunt and Nikki chose a silvery tiara studded with pink plastic jewels.

"There are Ruby and Lacey!" exclaimed Olivia as they left Bubble Gum. And sure enough, just several feet away was a group of velvet-clad carolers singing, *"Above thy deep and dreamless sleep the silent stars go by."*

Olivia, Nikki, and Flora listened until the song was finished, then waved to Ruby and Lacey, who removed their hands from their fake-fur muffs long enough to wave back.

"I guess it's time to go to Needle and Thread again," said Olivia, who had dutifully checked in with Gigi every half hour.

"Tobias is going to pick me up there soon," said Nikki.

The girls paused for one more look at the glittering Christmas tree in the square, grabbed one last chocolate from the bowl at Time and Again ("I'm beginning to feel a little sick," admitted Flora), and then returned to Needle and Thread, where Tobias was waiting.

As soon as he and Nikki left, Flora said to Olivia, "The surprise for the Shermans is going to be perfect, isn't it?"

"Perfect!" agreed Olivia. "I keep wanting to tell Nikki not to worry so much about Mae's gifts, but that would ruin everything. I don't want to spoil the surprise."

Olivia and Flora sprawled, groaning, on the couches at the front of the store. Presently, they were joined by Ruby, who said that the carolers had finished and were going home.

"Is there any food left?" Ruby wanted to know as she struggled with the fastenings on her boots.

Flora clutched her stomach. "How can you think of food?"

"I haven't eaten anything," said Ruby. "I've been singing all this time. I'm starving."

Ruby sat down with a plate of the little sandwiches that Min and Gigi had been serving (Olivia and Flora had to turn their heads away), and the girls watched as the crowds thinned and, one by one, the stores on Main Street grew dark. Gigi and Min were saying good night to their last customer when Mrs. Grindle strode through the door and dropped onto the couch next to Ruby.

"Oh, my aching feet," she said.

Ruby edged away from her and slid onto the other couch. Mrs. Grindle didn't seem to notice.

"Hi, Gina," called Min. "Long day?"

"I never," Mrs. Grindle replied.

Gigi ushered the customer out the door, turned the lock, set the CLOSED sign in the window, and sat beside Mrs. Grindle. Min joined them.

"I've come to a decision," said Mrs. Grindle briskly. She crossed her feet, then her arms.

"I bet her fingers and toes are crossed, too," Olivia whispered to Flora.

"I have decided," said Mrs. Grindle, "that after the

holidays are over, I'm going to put Stuff 'n' Nonsense up for sale."

Olivia turned a shocked face to her friends. She didn't like the Grinch, couldn't stand her, but Stuff 'n' Nonsense had been around since long before Olivia was born. It was part of Main Street, part of town, part of her life. And Olivia didn't want one more thing in her life to change.

"Oh, no," she whispered.

CHAPTER II

Aunt Allie

On December 20th, five days before Christmas, Ruby Northrop stood in front of the mirror in her room and gave herself a concert. *"On the fifth day of Christmas,"* she sang, even though she had a feeling that the fifth day of Christmas wasn't December 20th, *"my true love sent to me, five golden rings, four collie birds, three French hens, two turtle doves, and a partridge in a pear tree!"* What an odd song, she thought. Why is this true love giving away so many birds, and what's a collie bird anyway? Ruby checked the book of Christmas carols she had borrowed from Ms. Angelo. "Oh, *calling* bird," she said aloud. Then, "Well, what's a calling bird?"

"Ruby! Come downstairs for breakfast, please!" said Min.

"Okay." Ruby looked at the calendar on her wall. It was very strange, she thought, how time seemed to slow down before an important holiday, and the closer the holiday came, the slower time passed. How was she ever going to make it through today and tomorrow (the last two days of school before vacation), then an entire weekend, and then all of Monday, which was Christmas Eve, the longest day of the year? Well, they will be busy days, she reminded herself. She had a test at school on Friday (kind of mean of Mr. Lundy), but then a class party (nice of Mr. Lundy). She had her Christmas surprise to work on over the weekend, a rehearsal of the Children's Chorus for their performance on Monday, and she still had presents to wrap. Christmas Eve would be a very busy day, and then —

"Ruby! Lordy Maudy! What are you doing?" called Min. "Please come down to breakfast now!"

Ruby was well acquainted with this particular tone of voice and flew out of her bedroom and down to the kitchen. "Sorry, Min," she said as she slid into her chair.

"My goodness," said Min. "Now, girls, I want to remind you that your aunt Allie will be arriving at about four this afternoon. Ruby, you have a chorus rehearsal after school, is that right?"

"Yes," said Ruby.

"And, Flora, you'll be at the store, is that right?"

"Yes."

"Okay, then I think I'll ask Allie to come directly to Needle and Thread when she gets to town. The bus is due in at —"

"The bus?" said Ruby. "Isn't she driving? Doesn't she have a car?"

Min shook her head. "She lives in New York City. She doesn't need a car."

Ruby's mind turned to what she knew about her aunt. It wasn't much. Aunt Allie was her mother's younger sister. For some reason, her mother and Allie hadn't gotten along well. Ruby didn't think anything in particular had happened. The sisters just hadn't been close. Ruby couldn't imagine not being close to Flora, though. Flora was one of her very best friends.

Ruby's mother and Allie had grown up and gone to college (different colleges). After college, Ruby's mother had met Ruby's father and they had gotten married and moved to a town that was bigger than Camden Falls but nowhere near as big as New York City, which was where Allie had moved. Ruby thought she remembered her mother once saying that New York was one of Allie's phases, that she would live there for a while, then move somewhere smaller and closer by. Instead, Allie had had her first book published, a collection of short stories. "For grown-ups," Ruby's mother had said. And Allie had stayed in New York. Then she had written another book, and then a third and a fourth.

"Is Aunt Allie famous?" Ruby had once asked her mother.

"In some circles," was the reply, which Ruby hadn't understood at all. Circles?

The years had gone by, and Ruby's mother and Allie rarely saw each other. Ruby had met her aunt only a few times. Min, on the other hand, had remained closely in touch with Allie. Allie almost never visited Camden Falls, but for as long as Ruby could remember, Min had gone to New York City to spend Christmas with Allie.

And now everything had changed. Ruby's parents were gone, Min had decided not to go to New York on this first Christmas with Ruby and Flora, and Allie had decided to visit Camden Falls after so many years away.

Ruby realized she felt a bit afraid of her aunt.

"I hope Aunt Allie will like her room," she said now.

Min, Flora, and Ruby had worked hard to make one of the guest rooms on the third floor both cozy and festive. They had cleaned it (it hadn't been used in a very long time), put flannel sheets on the bed, made sure the little alarm clock was running, and had placed some books they thought she might like on the bedside table. Flora had even painted two pictures that were now hanging on the wall, and then Ruby had gotten the idea to decorate the room for Christmas. "We could put a little tree in the corner and string lights around the window," she'd said. And that was exactly what they'd done.

"I'm sure she'll love the room," said Min.

"Do you think she'll mind that she won't be staying

in her own old bedroom?" asked Ruby. "Do you think she'll mind that her old room is my room now?"

"Not at all," Min said. "Don't give that a second thought."

Ruby ate her breakfast quickly so she would have time for a ritual she had begun as soon as she and Min and Flora had decorated the house and put up their Christmas tree. She stood in the doorway to the living room and looked at the pine boughs over the picture frames, each one hung with tiny wooden angels, and the elaborate scene Min had created on the mantelpiece. She had placed pine boughs there, too, and nestled among the needles were antique tree ornaments ("Some of these belonged to my mother," Min had said), and a choir of brass angels, and a trio of gnomes from Norway, as well as holly berries and gold-painted pinecones and more wooden angels. Ruby surveyed the other decorations as well — a music box from a trip Min had taken to Germany, a large jointed wooden soldier, the kissing ball with its sprig of plastic mistletoe, and Min's impressive collection of Nativity scenes.

Ruby took in the entire room, then she closed her eyes. Her hand found the light switch, and she flicked it up. When she opened her eyes, the tree was lit. This wasn't quite as astonishing in the morning as it was in the evening with only darkness outside the windows, but Ruby couldn't help herself. She liked to do this twice a day. And she liked to examine the ornaments on the tree. There were Min's — new to Ruby — and there were the ones Flora and Ruby had brought from their old house. Ruby fingered the Santa on skis, the cat with the halo over his head (she thought of him as Halo Kitty), the miniature Nativity, the glass peacock.

"Is this the first time you've decorated the house since Aunt Allie moved to New York?" Ruby had asked Min.

"Oh, no," Min replied. "I decorate every year. I don't think I could *not* decorate. I get a tree and everything. Of course, when I went to the city, I would have to leave it all behind for a few days. Still, it would be waiting for me when I came home. I usually leave everything up until the week after New Year's. Then away it goes until the next December."

Ruby eyed the floor beneath the tree. Empty — except for a red-and-green tree skirt. Min had insisted on waiting until Aunt Allie arrived before putting out any presents. Ruby was getting impatient. She knew a few good secrets. One of the closets downstairs was now absolutely stuffed with gifts — with packages that had arrived in the mail or that friends had dropped off, and with presents Min had wrapped, as well as some Flora and Ruby had wrapped. At Ruby's old home, when her parents had been alive, presents had been placed under the tree as soon as the bows were tied, or as soon as the mail carrier delivered them. Ruby had to admit that the bursting closet was fairly exciting, though.

"Ruby!" Flora called. "We have to leave now or we're going to be late."

So off Ruby went for her second-to-last day of school before vacation. When she returned home at the end of the afternoon, her aunt Allie was there.

Ruby had had a long day. The chorus rehearsal lasted for two hours. But Ruby's spirits were high, and when she ran through the front door of the Row House at 5:15, she was singing loudly, *John Jacob Jingleheimer Schmidt! His name is my name, too!* (Ruby was a little tired of Christmas songs.) *Whenever we go out, the people always —*"

Ruby slammed the door shut behind her and came to a halt in the front hallway. Sitting in the living room were Min, Flora, and a woman Ruby recognized more from photos than from memory. She was tall, like Ruby's mother had been, and dark-haired and dark-eyed, also like Ruby's mother, but she was dressed in clothes that Ruby had never, ever seen her mother wear — tight faded jeans and a loose filmy top studded with things that looked like tiny mirrors, black lace-up boots, and lots of large jingly jewelry.

"My goodness," the woman said to Ruby. "That was quite an entrance."

Ordinarily, Ruby liked to make an entrance, but what her aunt Allie had just said didn't sound like a compliment, so Ruby lowered her backpack to the floor, hung up her coat, and approached the living room quietly. She held out her hand. "Hi, Aunt Allie," she said. "I'm Ruby."

"So I gather." Ruby's aunt stood up and shook her hand.

A brief silence followed. Finally, Ruby said, "We're very glad you could change your plans and join us for the holidays."

"Why, thank you," replied Aunt Allie.

"Well," said Min, standing up, "I'll go start dinner."

"I'll help you," said Aunt Allie.

"Come upstairs with me, Ruby," said Flora.

Flora fairly sprinted up the stairs to her room, and Ruby followed her.

"She's awful!" exclaimed Flora, as soon as she had closed her door. "Just awful! She has no sense of humor, I don't think she likes kids, and she seems kind of complainy."

"Complainy? How?" asked Ruby.

Flora made a face. "The bus was too hot, and Needle and Thread was too crowded, and she needs to work — she's on a deadline — but if she can't access the Internet here, then she's in big trouble."

"What makes you think she doesn't like kids?" asked Ruby nervously.

"She's hardly talked to me, and this afternoon I gave her a welcome card I made and she thanked me for it, but she studied it like she was looking for mistakes or something. Also, I overheard her ask Min if we have savings accounts so we can deposit her Christmas presents in them."

"Money to put into our savings accounts?" wailed Ruby. That was the most boring present imaginable. But maybe that would just be Aunt Allie's main present; maybe there would be others as well.

"And I bought her a pen for Christmas," continued Flora, "a nice pen, which I guess she won't use if she's so concerned about her computer. I have to say, it's a little hard to be in the holiday spirit right now."

Ruby and Flora turned up at the dinner table that night in very bad moods. They barely spoke, but Aunt Allie didn't seem to notice. She carried on a cheerful conversation with Min. After supper, Ruby finally did ask her a question. "How do you like our decorations?" she said as Aunt Allie sat down on the living room couch and turned on her laptop.

"What? Oh, the decorations are just fine. Very — oh, no, not *this* problem again. Where did I leave my power cord?"

At that moment, Ruby, knowing she shouldn't do it but unable to stop herself, flicked a switch that turned off all the lamps in the room and then flicked the switch that turned on the Christmas tree lights.

"Ruby!" cried Aunt Allie. "I can't see!"

"But the tree —" said Ruby.

Aunt Allie turned the lamps on again, and Ruby huffed upstairs to her bedroom.

CHAPTER 12

School's Out

"Just four more days! Just four more days!" Mae chanted as she and Nikki stepped off the school bus the next morning.

"Four more days until what?" Olivia teased. She and Flora and Ruby had been waiting in front of Camden Falls Elementary for the Shermans.

"Christmas, silly," said Mae. "And only three more nights until Santa Claus comes."

Nikki's backpack was heavier than usual, for this morning it held, in addition to her books, a handmade card for Mr. Donaldson and one for each of her classmates, cards that would be distributed that afternoon at their last-day-before-vacation party. Nikki was bursting with enthusiasm. The last day before vacation, a party, a special assembly, plans with Flora and Ruby and Olivia after school, Christmas in just four days — and no dad to spoil any of it.

Mr. Donaldson's party was held after lunch. When Nikki and her classmates returned to their room, they found that their teacher had cleared his desk of books and papers and pens and had spread a green paper tablecloth over it. The desk now held a bowl filled with red punch, a plate of cookies, a plate of cupcakes, a tower of plastic cups, and a stack of napkins. For half an hour, Nikki and her classmates walked around their room holding cookies over napkins, exchanging cards, chattering about their plans for vacation, and watching the snow that had started to fall.

When the food was gone and the chattering had died down, Mr. Donaldson looked at his watch and said, "Time for the assembly. Please line up at the door."

Nikki rushed to stand with Olivia and Flora. "Is Ruby excited?" she asked Flora.

"Yes. Even though our aunt couldn't care less about the play. Ruby tried to tell her about it last night, but I don't think Aunt Allie was listening at all."

The assembly, which was for the entire school, was a rehearsal of the play that was to be performed during the 350th birthday celebration, the one in which Ruby had the lead role, that of Alice Kendall, a seventeenth-century woman accused of being a witch.

"Welcome, boys and girls," said Mrs. Gillipetti, the director of the play, when the students had taken their seats in the auditorium. "As most of you know, we have been rehearsing for about two months now. We have a long way to go — we haven't even held a dress rehearsal yet — but we thought you'd like to see our progress."

Nikki admitted later (just to herself; she would never say this to her friends) that the play did indeed have a long way to go. The scenery, which was only partially painted, kept toppling over backward. The kindergartners never seemed to know where on the stage they should be, and one of them actually fell off the stage — then, to everyone's relief, simply stood up and ran back to his spot in the scene. And with one exception, every kid who could read was still using a playbook. It was, Nikki felt, a bit difficult to imagine this as a true play when the characters were wandering around in their school clothes, reading their lines from books. Only Ruby didn't carry a book. "I've already memorized all my lines," she had told Flora and Olivia and Nikki that morning.

This turned out not to be true.

In the second act, a boy named Jerry McCabe, who was playing Alice Kendall's neighbor John Parson, walked onto the stage (wearing his blue jeans and a Boston Bruins sweatshirt, and carrying his playbook) and read, "What is that perched on your house?"

Nobody on the stage answered him.

Jerry consulted his playbook again and then said more loudly, "What is that PERCHED on your HOUSE?" No response. He looked squarely at Ruby. "I SAID, WHAT IS THAT PERCHED ON YOUR HOUSE?"

Mrs. Gillipetti leaned onto the stage from the wings. "Ruby, dear, that's your cue."

"Oh!" said Ruby. She paused thoughtfully, then said, "Why, it's nothing but a crow, John Parson."

"Wouldn't you call it a familiar?" read Jerry.

"Um," said Ruby. "Um . . ."

This time only Mrs. Gillipetti's hand appeared from the wings. It held Ruby's playbook. Ruby took it and thumbed through it. She used the book for the remainder of the program. And she bravely ignored the giggling in the audience.

When the assembly ended, so did school. Nikki and her classmates walked through the hallways of Camden Falls Elementary as fast as they could without actually running.

"Vacation!" Nikki cried to Olivia and Flora.

"Christmas!" Olivia cried.

Flora said nothing, and Nikki reminded herself that this holiday was not going to be as joyous for Flora and Ruby as it would be for most of their friends. Nikki took Flora's hand and squeezed it, then let it drop when Flora began to smile and said, "I can't wait to deliver the presents this afternoon."

Nikki and Olivia and Flora gathered up their backpacks and coats, then called "Good-bye!" and "Happy Holidays!" to Mr. Donaldson and their classmates. Mr. Donaldson reminded everyone to read at least one book over vacation, and then Nikki was free. She and Flora and Olivia flew to the front door of their school and waited there for Ruby. The four friends ran most of the way to Main Street, catching snowflakes on their tongues as they went.

"Maybe we'll have a blizzard for Christmas!" cried Nikki.

"No, we don't want a snowstorm on Christmas Eve," said Ruby.

"Why not?" asked Nikki, as Olivia elbowed Ruby in the ribs.

"Here we are!" said Flora loudly. She opened the door to Needle and Thread. "Look, everything is ready."

Waiting by the couches at the front of the store were a number of bags filled with wrapped Christmas presents. Nikki looked at the bags proudly. Not only had she made several of the gifts, but she had helped to wrap them. Now they were going to be distributed with the day's Special Delivery meals. And Nikki, Flora, Olivia, and Ruby were going to accompany Mr. Pennington on his route.

"There's Mr. Pennington now!" exclaimed Ruby. She flung open the door as Mr. Pennington pulled up in front of the store. "We're ready! We're ready!" she called.

"Ruby, darling, you need to calm down just a teeny bit," Min said quietly.

Mr. Pennington entered the store with a smile on his face and a list in his hand. "Greetings," he said cheerfully. "I've already picked up the meals, girls. Now we need to find the right gifts." He held out the list. "We need the presents for these ten people."

In no time, the gifts had been located and the girls piled into Mr. Pennington's car.

"I didn't know Sonny Sutphin would be on the list," Nikki commented as Mr. Pennington set off down Main Street.

"I believe he's a new client," said Mr. Pennington. "At least, this is the first time he's been on my route. He lives nearby, so we'll go to his place first."

"I haven't been to Sonny's house before," said Olivia, sounding awed. "It's funny, but I never thought of him actually living somewhere. I just always see him on the street."

"It's like you never think of your teachers living anywhere because you only see them in school," said Flora.

Mr. Pennington had turned off Main Street and driven a couple of blocks to a road where the houses were small and crowded together, and paint was peeling, and here and there roofs were missing shingles.

They look kind of like my house, Nikki thought, and glanced at her friends. They were staring out the car windows. Nobody spoke.

Mr. Pennington parked his car in front of a pale blue house with a wooden Santa in the yard. There was a snowman, too, but it had fallen over and was leaning against a bush.

"I think his door is at the back of the house," said Mr. Pennington. "I'll get the meal out of the trunk. Who has Sonny's present?"

"I do," said Nikki.

"What if he's not at home?" asked Olivia. "Isn't he usually in town?"

"I think he'll be here," said Mr. Pennington.

A few moments later, Nikki knocked on the back door of the house. She heard a small thump and then the door was opened by Sonny Sutphin.

"Merry Christmas," said Mr. Pennington heartily.

Sonny grinned. "Merry Christmas! I didn't expect a whole party. Looky here, it's Flora and Ruby and Olivia and — are you Nikki?"

Nikki nodded, then held out the present. "This is for you."

"For me? A gift for me?" Sonny's grin widened. "Please come in," he said, backing up his chair. "Won't you come in for a visit?"

"We'd love to," said Mr. Pennington, "although I'm afraid we'll have to keep it short. Here, let me put this in your refrigerator, Mr. Sutphin. It's a complete dinner, as well as some food for the weekend. All you have to do is heat up the dinner in the oven. No cooking involved."

Nikki stepped through the doorway and into Sonny's apartment. It consisted, as far as she could see, of two rooms. The room in which she was now standing was a sitting room with a kitchen at one end. Through a doorway, Nikki glimpsed a small bedroom. She looked around for decorations and saw that Sonny had hung a cardboard wreath in one of his windows.

Sonny set the present on the table. "I'm going to wait until Christmas Day to open this," he said.

"It's handmade," Ruby informed him.

"That's the best kind."

Mr. Pennington asked Sonny if he planned to go to the Christmas Eve festivities on Main Street, and then Ruby invited him to her concert. "It's at the community center," she said. "Two o'clock."

"Well," said Mr. Pennington a moment later, "we should be on our way."

"So soon?" asked Sonny.

"I'm afraid so."

The rest of the afternoon was spent driving from one home to another. Nikki and her friends visited with people who were sick and a woman who was blind and a couple who reminded Nikki of Mr. and Mrs. Willet, except it was the husband who was confused and forgetful. The woman who was blind burst into quiet tears when Olivia handed her the wrapped gift. The man who was confused wanted to open his present right away, and when his wife said okay, he set the package down, went off in search of a pair of scissors, and forgot about the present.

The next-to-last house they visited belonged to a man who sounded very old, but no one got to see him. Mr. Pennington knocked on his door, and an irritated voice called, "Who is it?"

"Special Delivery!" replied Mr. Pennington.

"Well, leave it where you always do."

Nikki frowned. "We have a present for you, too," she said.

"Good."

"Don't you —" Flora started to say, but Mr. Pennington shushed her.

"Merry Christmas, Mr. Crasden!" he called.

At the last stop, the door was opened by a woman leaning on a walker. She accepted the meal and the gift with tears in her eyes, and as her visitors were leaving, she pressed chocolates into their hands and told them they were her Christmas angels.

Mr. Pennington drove Nikki to her house after that, and as she ran to her front door, she felt grateful for Mae and her mother and Tobias and each small reminder of Christmas that would be waiting for her inside.

CHAPTER 13

Mary's Christmas

Each time Flora Marie Northrop walked to Mary Woolsey's house, she remembered her first visit to the little cottage in June, when Mary's yard, which was really just one enormous garden with a house in the middle, had been lush and colorful, alive with flowers and insects and birds. Now the house was a drab island in a sea of snow.

"*Brr,*" Flora couldn't help saying as she made her way along the path to Mary's front door. More snow was falling, and Flora's toes were turning numb.

But Flora didn't mind. She was holding a small bag in one hand, and every time she thought about its contents (a lacy pink-and-green sachet handmade by Flora), she felt a thrill of excitement and happiness.

"Can I come see you tomorrow?" she had asked Mary at Needle and Thread the day before.

Mary had replied, "You certainly may. A Christmas visit. Lovely."

Flora noted that Mary's walk was tidily shoveled, and that a wreath of holly hung in each window. She had a feeling that Mary had made the wreaths herself.

"Merry Christmas!" called Mary suddenly, opening her door with a flourish.

"Merry Christmas!" Flora replied.

"Come in out of the cold. You must be freezing."

Flora stepped into the cottage and removed her boots and coat. She held the gift bag out to Mary. "This is for you," she said.

Mary took the bag, which was red and decorated with a picture of wrens holding ornaments in their beaks and fluttering around a shimmering woodland Christmas tree. "Thank you, Flora," said Mary. She smiled. "Don't you wish things like this really happened at Christmastime?"

"Things like what?"

Mary pointed to the bag. "Like this." She indicated the birds decorating the tree. "Magical things."

"Maybe they do," said Flora.

"And we just don't see them," agreed Mary. "Come, sit down."

Flora followed Mary Woolsey into the parlor. "Oh!" she exclaimed. She didn't know why she was surprised to find that Mary had decorated the inside of her house for Christmas, but she was. Flora was standing before one of the most beautiful trees she had ever seen. And that wasn't all. Garlands wound with ribbons were draped over each window. A parade of angels marched across the mantelpiece. Mary had even hung a miniature wreath on the door of the cuckoo clock.

Mary looked fondly at the tree. "Do you like it? I saved all the ornaments my mother and I collected when I was a little girl. And I've been collecting ever since. Making ornaments, too. See those snowflakes? They're crocheted. And my mother and I made those beaded ornaments."

"Ooh," said Flora. The tree glittered, its branches weighed down with hundreds of gold lights, with tinsel, with tin soldiers and wooden jumping jacks and tiny Nativity scenes — one so small it had been carved into half of a walnut shell — and colored glass balls and birds with tails of spun glass. There was also a miniature bird feeder, a miniature sewing case, a miniature castle, and a teeny, tiny hummingbird.

Flora didn't know what to say, so she just let out a sigh.

"We didn't have much money when I was growing up, but my mother made Christmas special. It's still special," Mary explained.

"Do you want to open your present now?" asked Flora.

"Well," said Mary, "if you don't mind, I like to save

all my presents for Christmas Day. But you can open yours now." She reached under the tree, where a handful of gifts was scattered, selected a small one wrapped in silver and tied with a pale blue ribbon, and gave it to Flora.

"Thank you," said Flora, feeling suddenly shy. "I think I'll save mine for Christmas, too." Who, Flora wondered, would Mary celebrate with on Christmas Day?

The clock began to chime then, and the wreath-bedecked door flew open, launching the cuckoo out of his house.

Mary looked at the clock. "Time for Christmas tea," she said. "You sit here with the cats. I'll be back in just a moment."

Flora, her mind on Mary's Christmas, sat on the edge of an armchair where Daphne and Delilah, the two orange cats, slept soundly, entwined in each other's legs. Flora patted them until they rumbled with purrs, and finally Daphne opened one eye and looked sleepily at Flora. "Hi, Daphne," said Flora, and Daphne closed the eye.

When Mary returned to the parlor, she was carrying a tray, which she set on the table in front of the couch. "Have you ever had Christmas tea?" she asked.

"I don't think so." Flora sniffed the air. "It smells spicy."

"It is. And," said Mary, "this is how you stir it. No spoon needed, no sugar, either." She dropped a peppermint stick into one of the cups and handed it to Flora. "Use this."

"Peppermint candy!" exclaimed Flora. She thought Mary was one of the cleverest people she knew.

When the peppermint had melted away, and Flora and Mary were sipping their tea and daintily chewing Mary's ginger cookies, Mary said, "How's the research coming?"

Flora swallowed dryly. "I haven't . . . With the holidays and everything . . ." She cleared her throat.

"You haven't been doing much research?" asked Mary with a smile.

"No," Flora admitted. She thought about her history project, the one Olivia had mentioned to Mr. Donaldson when he had asked about the 350th birthday festivities. Flora had learned that her great-grandfather, Lyman Davis (Min's father), who had been a stockbroker, had quit his job after the great stock market crash of 1929. He had quit because so many of his clients blamed him for losing their fortunes, and maybe, thought Flora, he truly had lost their fortunes. Or maybe he hadn't. In any case, his actions set in motion events that would alter the course of the lives of many people in Camden Falls — including Mary's. Flora had thought and thought about this and realized that perhaps some people's lives had changed for the better. Or in unpredictable ways. It was possible. Flora couldn't simply say that because of Min's father lots of people lost their money and their homes and had to start over. It was much more complicated than that.

Flora had started to think about history, and about how the smallest thing could affect bigger things and have consequences that reverberated for generations, maybe forever. One day, for instance, you're talking to a friend you run into in the street, and you talk longer than you intended, so now that person is running late and, because of that, doesn't stop in at the coffee shop (where normally he stops every day) and therefore misses meeting the person he might have married. (Tragic, tragic, thought Flora.) On the other hand, a simple missed meeting could prevent a catastrophe or a war.

So, Flora reasoned, wasn't it possible that some unexpectedly good things came from her great-grandfather's actions? This wasn't necessarily the thrust of her project, though. She just wanted to know what had happened, good or bad, and she figured that plenty of people in Camden Falls had stories to tell, as Mary did. Flora thought she might find several of these people and interview them. It would be an interesting slice of Camden Falls history and perfect material for the town birthday festivities.

"I've read all the letters about Lyman Davis that I found in our attic," Flora told Mary, "and I have a general idea of what happened after nineteen twenty-nine.

But I want more personal stories. Like yours. It's really interesting to know what happened to people, even if it isn't all good."

"In my case," said Mary, "it led to a mystery."

"Yes!" said Flora. "So there must be other stories. I should talk to Min again. But she'll only be able to help a little because she wasn't even born until several years after the crash. She doesn't remember a lot of things, like the years when your mother worked for her parents."

"You need to find some real old-timers," said Mary. "People who are older than Min. You know, one person you might want to talk to is Mrs. Fitzpatrick. I don't think you know her. I do lots of sewing for her, but she doesn't come into Needle and Thread very often. The Fitzpatricks are quite wealthy, but it seems to me that wasn't always so. I believe that the family lost money in nineteen twenty-nine. Whether it was because of your great-grandfather, I don't know. But Mrs. Fitzpatrick would be an interesting person to talk to. And she might tell you about some other people you could interview."

"Okay," said Flora. "Thank you." She took a final swallow of peppermint-laced tea, and for a moment gazed at the ornaments on Mary's tree. "What about you?" she asked. "Have you found out anything more about your benefactor?"

"Not exactly," said Mary, "but I did hear an

interesting bit of information on TV the other day. Earlier I'd been going through my mother's papers again, looking for clues, and suddenly I remembered something my mother had told me years and years ago. I was about twelve, I suppose, and I had asked Mother why we never visited my father's grave. It was some holiday or other — I don't remember which one — and I wanted to put flowers on his grave. I had just read about that custom in a book and it occurred to me that we had never gone to the cemetery. A very strange look crossed my mother's face when I asked that question, and after a moment she said my father didn't have a grave. I asked her why, and she replied that his remains hadn't been found, so there was nothing to bury."

"Why couldn't you have had a gravestone for your father, even if nothing was buried there?" asked Flora.

"A very good question," said Mary, "but one I didn't know enough to ask. Then, the other day, I was watching a true-crime show, and I learned that although most people think a fire is a good way to cover up a crime — you know, set fire to a house to hide the fact that a murder was committed there — it isn't. And this is because fire almost never burns a body completely." Flora shivered, and Mary said, "I know. It's unpleasant — and certainly not very Christmasy. But it was important because it made me wonder why nothing was ever found of my father. The newspaper articles I read about the factory fire mentioned identifying the workers by their remains. So what happened to my father's remains? I set out looking for my benefactor, and instead, my father's death became another mystery."

"But back then," said Flora, "there weren't any crime labs. I mean, you couldn't identify people by their DNA like you can today. Isn't it possible there were remains of your father, but nobody knew how to identify them?"

"I suppose so," said Mary. "Still, that doesn't explain why my mother decided not to put up a headstone in his memory. She could have buried something symbolic or meaningful, such as ashes from the fire." It was Mary's turn to shiver and she set down her teacup. "My goodness. Such talk. Let's put it aside. Tell me, Flora, how are you going to celebrate the holidays?"

Flora told Mary their plans for the next few days, including Ruby's concert and the surprise for Mae Sherman on Christmas Eve. A few minutes later, Mary rose, and Flora stood, too.

"Thank you for the visit," said Mary.

And Flora, without knowing she was going to say anything, blurted out, "Would you like to come over on Christmas Day?"

"Oh, no, dear. Thank you very much."

"Will you have visitors then?"

"No," said Mary simply. "I'm used to celebrating alone."

Flora, who had been feeling rather sorry for herself, facing her first Christmas without her parents, now tried to imagine celebrating the day with no one at all and couldn't do it. But Mary, standing in her parlor amid her tree and her cats, a fire blazing in the hearth, looked serene and not at all sad. So Flora hugged her, wished her a merry Christmas, and walked outside. There was wood smoke in the air, peppermint on her tongue, and a gift in her hand. She turned for a final look at the peaceful house and set out for her own home.

CHAPTER 14

Secrets

"Doll?"

"Check!"

"Doll clothes?"

"Check."

"Stuffed dog?"

"Check."

"Piano?"

"Check."

The items Mae Sherman had asked Santa for (as well as several things she hadn't requested) were arranged in Olivia's living room. And Olivia was standing over them, clipboard in hand.

"We did it!" she said. "With a lot of help."

"Everyone was so generous," said Flora.

"Presents for all the Shermans," added Ruby. "Well, except for Mr. Sherman."

Olivia and her friends had worked hard. They had talked to Olivia's parents and Min and their friends, young and old, and had collected enough money for a truly special Christmas surprise for Mae and Nikki and their family. The day before, Olivia, Flora, and Ruby had gone into town and headed first to Zinder's to buy exactly what Mae had requested — a doll with party clothes, a stuffed dog (not as big as Paw-Paw but still quite large), a bead kit, and a small but playable piano. (Nikki had already purchased Twister and the crayons.) Then, just for fun, and because they could afford it, they had bought another set of clothes for the doll and a stack of paper to go with the crayons.

After that, they set out for Cover to Cover, where they chose books for everyone in the family. Olivia was in charge of Mrs. Sherman (who she didn't know at all), and after much consideration chose *To Kill a Mockingbird* for her, a book she knew her own mother liked. Flora had the hardest job, choosing something for Tobias. She thought and thought and looked and looked and finally, after consulting with Ms. Vinsel (one of the owners of the store) chose *The Lord of the Rings* trilogy. Ruby's job was the easiest and the most fun (in her opinion). She was to buy books for Nikki and Mae, and chose two for each — *The Saturdays* and *A Wrinkle in Time* for Nikki, and *A Bear Called Paddington* and *The Polar Express* for Mae.

"These bags are heavy!" Olivia had exclaimed as

they left the bookstore, so they walked to Needle and Thread and hid the packages in the storeroom.

"Now where should we go?" asked Ruby.

"How about Flare?" suggested Flora. "Their clothes aren't too expensive, and we could get something for everyone."

So Flare was the girls' next stop. They chose a party dress for Mae (guessing at her size), two shirts for Nikki, and scarves for Tobias and Mrs. Sherman.

"How much money do we have left?" asked Ruby as they left Flare with a bulging shopping bag.

Olivia counted the bills in an envelope that she had labeled SECRET SANTA. "A little over a hundred dollars," she said.

"Excellent!" said Flora. "Let's get a couple more things for Nikki and Tobias and Mrs. Sherman and then buy the extras."

The "extras" were wrapping paper, a box of candy canes, and food for Christmas dinner.

They needed help when it came time to buy the food, so Mr. Walter drove the girls to the grocery store and selected some of the more difficult items for them, such as the turkey.

At the end of the day, when everything — toys and books and clothes and food — had been stowed at the Walters', all Olivia could say was, "Wow." This, however, was before Olivia's mother called from Stuff 'n' Nonsense and asked if Olivia's father could come to the store at closing time. Olivia, sensing something out of the ordinary, begged to go along, so in the end, the entire Walter family gathered in the store.

"Gina," said Olivia's mother, with a nod at Mrs. Grindle, "wants to propose something."

Mrs. Grindle closed her eyes briefly, then said, "I can't believe I'm about to say this, but . . . I'm thinking of selling the store. Lately, it's just seemed too difficult to manage. But it would be a great relief to me to know that if I did decide to sell it, you'd be interested in buying it."

Olivia's mother looked at her husband. "It isn't exactly what we're looking for," she said.

"It doesn't have a kitchen," said Mr. Walter.

"But maybe we could make it work."

"And it's right here in town!" exclaimed Olivia, trying not to shriek.

"We'll think about it," said Mr. Walter.

"Then I can breathe easier," said Mrs. Grindle.

Me, too, thought Olivia, who spent the rest of Saturday evening feeling very giddy.

And now it was Sunday and time to turn her attention back to the surprise for Nikki.

"Let's go over the plans again," said Flora as the girls settled onto the Walters' living room floor with tape and scissors and paper and ribbon, ready to wrap the gifts.

"Okay," said Olivia. "Tomorrow night —"

"I can't believe tomorrow is actually Christmas Eve," said Ruby dreamily.

"Tomorrow night after the Christmas parade," Olivia continued, "around six o'clock, everyone who's going to the Shermans' —"

"Sorry to interrupt," said Flora, "but remind me who's going. Tell me everybody."

"My parents and Henry and Jack," replied Olivia, "and Min. Is your aunt coming?" (Flora and Ruby shrugged.) "Well, okay. And Mr. Willet, of course." (Mr. Willet was going to be Santa Claus.) "And Mr. Pennington."

"I think Lacey wants to go, too," said Ruby.

"And Lacey," said Olivia. "Anyway, we'll meet back here after the parade, and we'll load everything into our van. Mom and Dad will drive the van to Nikki's, and Henry and Jack and I will ride with Mr. Pennington."

"Mr. Willet and Lacey can ride with us," said Flora. "Mr. Willet will already have the Santa costume on, by the way."

"Okay. We should park at the end of the Shermans' lane, and then we'll carry everything to their house. We'll do it really quietly. I hope Paw-Paw doesn't hear us and start barking. We'll put all the things on their front porch and then we'll hide, except for Mr. Willet. He'll stay there and we'll ring bells while he calls 'Ho, ho, ho' and stuff until the Shermans hear him. Then they'll open the door —"

"And Mae will get to see Santa!" cried Ruby.

When the presents had been wrapped, the girls regarded them with satisfaction.

"This is so exciting!" said Flora.

"My heart is dancing," said Ruby.

And suddenly Olivia could no longer keep her secret. "You guys," she said. "Guess what."

"What?" said Flora and Ruby.

"You have to promise not to tell anyone yet. Except Nikki."

"I promise," said Flora.

"I promise," said Ruby.

Olivia lowered her voice. "Mom and Dad," she said, "are thinking about buying Stuff 'n' Nonsense and starting their own business."

"Really?" said Flora.

"You're kidding!" exclaimed Ruby.

Olivia grinned. "Nope. They want to start selling their gift baskets." (Olivia refrained from mentioning that her parents had been looking at property in other towns.) "And Mrs. Grindle says she wants to give up the store. It would be perfect for Mom and Dad. Well, not perfect because they really need a place with a kitchen. But they think they could make it work."

"Cool," said Ruby.

"Wow," said Flora.

Olivia felt just the teensiest bit guilty for not telling her friends the whole story, but she didn't want to worry them. Not so close to Christmas. Besides, this possibility was so exciting that it had wiped away most of her own worries. She chose to ignore the small part of her brain that wondered whether Mrs. Grindle would actually give up the store.

Ruby lay down on the floor with her head under the Walters' Christmas tree. "Mmm, smell that," she said. "I could go to sleep right now and pretend I'm in a pine forest."

"Well, don't go to sleep," said Flora. "We were going to deliver the other presents, remember?"

"Oh," said Ruby with a groan. "I can't. I'm too tired."

"But the sled," said Olivia. "Think of the sled."

Ruby rolled out from under the tree. "Okay."

For nearly a week, Olivia, Ruby, and Flora had been planning to load the Walters' sled with presents for their neighbors and walk from one end of the row to the other, delivering them. They had been working hard making the gifts, and delivering them was part of the fun.

"We can pretend we're pioneers," said Olivia, "and the sled is our only way of getting around in the snow."

"And we can go caroling at each house!" added Ruby, suddenly inspired.

"No!" cried Flora. "I am not singing in public. Come on. We'd better get going."

Soon enough, the sled was piled with gifts. Olivia,

who had taken photos of her neighbors all year long, had printed them out and made frames for them, one for each family. Flora had done a lot of knitting, including a long striped scarf for Robby. Ruby's projects, in Olivia's opinion, ranged from ambitious (she had invented a board game for the Morris kids) to haphazard. The haphazard gifts included a hastily scrawled card for Mr. Pennington and a pencil cup she had created for Dr. Malone by wrapping a piece of construction paper around an empty soup can and printing MERRY CHRISTMAS! on it.

Olivia and her friends set off in daylight and returned after dusk, their sled now laden with gifts from their neighbors. Flora was red-cheeked and smiling, Ruby was singing *Frosty the snowman was a jolly, happy soul!*" and Olivia, her belly full of hot cider and cookies, was so gladdened by the sight of her house — Christmas tree in the window, lights twinkling around the front door, smoke curling out of the chimney — that she thought she might burst.

CHAPTER 15

Jolly Old St. Nick

When Flora was eight years old, she had decided that her favorite day of the year was Christmas Eve. Christmas Day was wonderful, but it always went by too fast. And when it was over, suddenly the holidays seemed stale, even if the rest of vacation stretched ahead of you, and even if you had a houseful of new toys to play with. The letdown was terrible. But on Christmas Eve you could still look forward to Christmas. And when you were little, you could dream about Santa's visit that night. Flora used to hope that Christmas Eve would go on and on forever. She thought she wouldn't even mind if Christmas Day never arrived, because the best part of Christmas was waiting for it.

But Flora wasn't eight anymore. She was eleven — almost twelve — and this would be the first time in her life that she had celebrated Christmas without her parents. She was worried about how this would feel (even though she and Min and Ruby had had many conversations about it), so when she went to bed the night before Christmas Eve, she tried playing a game. When you wake up tomorrow, she said to herself, pretend that Camden Falls is where you have always lived and always celebrated Christmas. Pretend that you have woken up in this room every single day, with Ruby across the hall and Min down the hall and Aunt Allie upstairs. And every morning you have looked out the window and seen Aiken Avenue. And every Christmas Eve morning you have thought, Yippee! Tonight is the parade on Main Street, and tomorrow Ruby and Min and Aunt Allie and I will celebrate Christmas.

Of course, this hadn't worked. When Flora awoke on Monday morning, the morning of her favorite day of all, her heart didn't leap as it had the year before. Instead, she felt a vague heaviness, so she lay in bed longer than usual. She watched the gray morning light slide into her room around the window shade, and she felt King Comma purring next to her head. She thought about Ruby's concert with the Children's Chorus that afternoon and the surprise for the Shermans, but nothing made her want to get out of bed.

She was still lying there (stewing, as Min would say) when the door to her room opened quietly and Ruby poked her head around it. "Flora?" she whispered.

"Yeah?"

"You're awake?"

"Yup."

"Well, why don't you get up? It's Christmas Eve."

Flora said nothing.

"Are you sick?" asked Ruby. "You can't be sick on Christmas."

"I'm not sick."

Ruby sat on the end of Flora's bed. "Are you sad?"

"Yes."

"So am I."

Flora raised herself on one elbow. "Really? You haven't seemed sad."

"I'm excited and sad at the same time. That's possible, you know."

"I know."

"Are you excited and sad, too, or just sad?" asked Ruby earnestly.

Flora thought for a moment about Mae and Santa Claus and remembered the fun of shopping at Zinder's and of delivering presents on the sled. Then she tried to imagine the parade on Main Street. She had never seen the parade, of course, but she had heard plenty about it. After the parade, Santa Claus arrived in town and not just waving from the last float. No, the method of his arrival was magical and unexpected and different every year. No one (except the mayor) knew who played Santa; it was a big Camden Falls secret. And no one knew how he would appear. Min said that once Santa had sprung out of a giant jack-in-the-box in the town square, and once he had been flown in on a helicopter, and once he had even ridden down Main Street on an elephant. Flora tried to picture this.

"Flora?" said Ruby.

"I guess I'm excited and sad," said Flora. Then she added, "I was thinking about the parade."

Ruby scooted closer to Flora and pulled King Comma into her lap. "How do you think Santa Claus will arrive tonight?" she asked.

Flora pursed her lips. "In a limo!" she said after a moment.

Ruby laughed. "I think someone's going to unwrap a gigantic present, and he'll be inside."

"Oh, that's good," said Flora. "Speaking of which, Min said we can put our presents under the tree today."

"The closet is stuffed," observed Ruby.

"I know some secrets!"

"Me, too."

And with that, Flora threw back the covers and leaped out of bed.

The Children's Chorus concert was held at the community center that afternoon, and when Flora walked inside with Aunt Allie — Min and Mr. Pennington arm in arm behind them — she drew in her breath. Pine boughs adorned the end of every row of seats, and garlands outlined each window. The room smelled as much like an evergreen forest as if Flora were actually walking through one. Tall white candles burned at the front of the room, and later, when the members of the chorus, wearing blue robes, filed solemnly from the back of the room to the risers at the front, each was carrying a candle in a tin holder, and their faces glowed in a golden light.

The room at this moment was hushed. Flora was sitting between Aunt Allie and Min, and she reached for Min's hand. Min gave it a squeeze, and Flora thought Min's eyes looked awfully bright. At the front of the room was a piano, but it was silent. There was not a sound until the first member of the chorus reached the risers. Then the choir began to sing "Silent Night." When the carol was over, the children, robes rustling, stood in tidy lines, their eyes on Ms. Angelo, who stood before them, also wearing a robe.

The next carol was "I Saw Three Ships," and Flora's gaze drifted from Ruby and Lacey to the windows and beyond. No snow was falling, not today, but the afternoon was overcast, and the light outside was silvery. Flora shivered. She looked at Min, whose eyes were still bright, then at her aunt, who seemed far away, even though she was just inches from Flora.

The program, Flora thought, was nearly perfect. After the first verse of "The Cherry Tree Carol," a boy in the second row started the second verse too early and sang "*As they —*" quite loudly and all alone before realizing his mistake (which made several of the choir members giggle), and just as the final notes of "O Christmas Tree" were being sung, a small girl stumbled off the end of the lowest riser. But the rest of the performance went off without a hitch, and after Ms. Angelo had thanked everyone for coming, the audience burst into applause.

It was when Flora rose to leave that she felt the little spark she always felt at this time on Christmas Eve, the spark that told her that magic was taking place, that now anything at all might happen. If only there really were a Santa Claus to slide down the chimney. If only animals truly did talk at midnight. If only she could somehow see the miracle that had taken place in the stable all those long years ago.

The magic was around her, and Flora did a little skip and impulsively took Min's hand and Mr. Pennington's as they collected Ruby and left the center.

"Back home now," said Min, the dusk gathering around them. "We have to put on our warmest clothes for the parade."

The air was raw and a wind whipped up and for a moment Flora thought she felt the prick of snowflakes on her cheek. At home, she and Ruby and Min and Aunt Allie wrapped themselves in down jackets and mufflers and donned boots and mittens and hats.

Then they called for Mr. Pennington and walked into town together.

"Wow," said Aunt Allie as they turned onto Main Street. "This brings back memories."

"The last parade I saw," said Min, "was the year before you moved to New York City."

"I haven't missed a parade since I was a kid," said Mr. Pennington. "I was fourteen and I caught a cold and my mother wouldn't let me come into town. Oh, I was mad at her."

"There's Olivia!" called Ruby. "Let's stand with Olivia."

Flora didn't know how her sister had spotted the Walters in the crowds of people that were lining the street. The bustling activity reminded her of the night the tree had been lit in the square — a blur of hats and heads and waving arms and babies riding on shoulders, of shouts and laughter and greetings and cries of "Merry Christmas!" The Row House neighbors stood together, and the adults eased the children toward the street so they could see better. Everyone kept craning their necks to the right, and Flora looked with them. Suddenly, she heard Robby say, "I see it! Here comes the parade!" and the crowd grew quieter.

From the south end of town came a pair of head-lights. As the lights drew closer, Flora saw six elves (they were not wearing coats, and must have been freezing) dancing along in front of a float. They were tossing chocolates into the crowd and heralding the arrival of a string quartet seated sedately on the float, playing "I'll Be Home for Christmas." Ruby jumped up and down and shouted, caught four chocolates, and gave two of them to Flora.

Flora took in a dizzying array of images after that — horses dressed as reindeer, the advanced tap class from Ruby's dance school tappety-tapping to "Jingle Bell Rock" on a float called Twelve Tappers Tapping, an enormous snowman who bounced down the street and frightened Alyssa Morris, a float on which Santa's workshop had come to life, and finally a fire truck out-lined in blinking red and white lights.

The fire truck was at the end of the parade. After it went by, everyone peered expectantly all around.

"Santa could be anywhere," said Robby, looking up and down Main Street and then above his head.

Flora looked to the sky, too, and that was when she thought she saw lights over the trees behind Cover to Cover.

"What's that?" she cried, pointing.

Everyone's attention was drawn to the sky. Flora stared fixedly, feeling like Dorothy watching Glinda's bubble grow larger as it floated over Munchkinland.

"It's a balloon!" Flora exclaimed to Ruby. "A hot air balloon!"

And it was. Flora now saw that a balloon, aglow in

lights, was hovering above Main Street. It wasn't a real balloon, Flora realized, for it was suspended from a crane that must have been parked in the alley between Cover to Cover and Fig Tree restaurant. But that didn't matter. On this magical night, it could have been real.

The balloon was lowered toward the ground. When it was not more than a few feet above Flora's head, she heard a shout, and then Santa rose from the basket of the balloon and began to wave to the crowd. Moments later, the balloon came to a gentle rest near the sidewalk, and Santa, still waving, opened a door in the basket, stepped out, and walked all the way down Main Street to cheers and clapping.

Flora looked over her shoulder at Min. "That," she said, "was fantastic."

CHAPTER 16

Jingle Bells

Ruby had never seen anything like Santa Claus floating to earth in a hot air balloon. Never, ever, ever. And she had been to the Thanksgiving Day parade in New York City *and* to Six Flags Great Adventure. And the evening wasn't over yet. Now it was time to surprise Mae, something Ruby had been looking forward to for several weeks.

Ruby and her family and the Row House neighbors, fully satisfied by the parade, walked slowly back to Aiken Avenue.

"I think I'll skip the next part," said Aunt Allie as they turned up their front walk.

"You're not coming to the Shermans' with us?" asked Ruby.

There was a pause. "I'll see you when you get back."

Aunt Allie disappeared inside and Ruby told

herself not to care. There was too much to do. She couldn't bother about . . . she tried to think of some kind way to describe her aunt (since it was Christmas Eve) and came up with "a shy person."

"All right, let's load up the van," called Olivia from next door. In no time the van was filled with the food and the wrapped presents. It looked, Ruby thought, like Santa's sleigh (if you squinted your eyes and ignored the roof and windows and tires).

Olivia and her brothers climbed into Mr. Pennington's car then, and Lacey and Mr. Willet crowded into Min's car. (Mrs. Morris had volunteered to look after Mrs. Willet.)

"You are a very realistic Santa," said Ruby approvingly.

"It's the suit," Mr. Willet replied.

"No, you're much better than a department store Santa. Isn't he, Flora?"

"Definitely."

Mr. Willet was as round as Ruby thought Santa should be, and he had white hair, and although he didn't have an actual beard, his fake one blended in quite nicely with his hair. You could barely see the elastic band over his ears.

Min steered the car through Camden Falls and then onto the country road to the Shermans' house. Behind her were the Walters and Mr. Pennington.

"We're a Christmas convoy," said Ruby. "Let's sing!"

So they sang "Feliz Navidad," which was Lacey's suggestion. (Flora sang very, very softly.)

"All right," said Min after a while. "I think we're getting close."

Ruby and Flora recognized the end of the lane that led to Nikki's house, and Min parked there with Mr. Pennington and Mrs. Walter pulling up behind her.

"Now," said Olivia, "we have to carry everything from here. Be very, very, very quiet. Oh, I *hope* Paw-Paw won't bark. Does everyone know what to do when we get to the house?"

Everyone did, and soon their arms were piled with bundles. They made their way along the lane, a silent procession in the stillness and the dark. Ruby felt a little nervous as her feet encountered stones and other obstacles in the snowy road, but she kept her eyes on the friendly lights of Nikki's house, which she could see in the distance.

Ruby was carrying a stack of presents (she thought they were Mae's doll and some of the books), and she followed Olivia to the Shermans' porch, where she placed the gifts soundlessly into a pack that Mr. Willet was holding open. Then she stepped off the porch and into the shadows, joining Flora, Min, Mr. Pennington, Lacey, and Olivia and her family. Mr. Willet remained by the door with the bulging pack. In the light from the Shermans' windows, Ruby could see that he was smiling — a jolly, rosy-cheeked Santa.

Mr. Willet nodded toward his hidden neighbors, and then, "Ho! Ho! Ho!" he bellowed. "Ho! Ho! Ho!"

Ruby pulled a cowbell out of her coat pocket and jangled it loudly. Olivia did the same and Flora shook the tiny bells that usually hung on King Comma's collar.

"Ho! Ho! Ho!" cried Mr. Willet again.

The Shermans' porch light flickered on, and a moment later Mae's face appeared in a window, curious, then awestruck. She turned around and called over her shoulder to someone behind her, and then the door flew open. There stood Mae, clinging to Nikki's hand, Tobias and Mrs. Sherman behind them.

"Ho! Ho! Ho! Merry Christmas!" said Mr. Willet.

Mae stared. She stared hard for nearly ten seconds (which is a very long time if you sit still and count it out). Then a grin crossed her face and she bounced up and down and began to shriek. "It's Santa! Mommy, Nikki, Tobias, it's Santa Claus! He came for real! I told you he would!"

Mr. Willet knelt on the porch. He appeared to study Mae. Then he consulted a long piece of paper that he withdrew from a pocket of his red coat.

"Are you Mae Sherman?" he asked her.

"Yes," Mae said anxiously, and then added, "sir."

"Just checking." Mr. Willet put the list away and opened the pack. "I have quite a few things in here for you," he said. "I think I have everything you requested. And presents for your sister and brother and mother, too."

"Presents for *every*body?!" exclaimed Mae.

Mr. Willet pulled out the list again, stared at it, then replaced it. "Yup."

Ruby looked at Nikki, still holding Mae's hand, and saw Nikki's eyes travel off the porch and into the darkness beyond.

Mr. Willet lifted one of the presents out of the pack and handed it to Mae. "This one is for you," he said, reading its tag. He pulled out another gift, then another and another and another, until the pack was empty and Mae stood by a tower of presents.

Mae gazed wide-eyed at Mr. Willet. "Oh, thank you!" she said finally. "Thank you. I didn't know that you could bring *all* the things on the list. Or that you would bring presents for everyone else. Was it the map?" she asked finally. "You just needed the map? Is that how you found me?"

"Well," said Mr. Willet, looking over his shoulder, "I did have a little help."

Out of the shadows stepped Ruby and Flora and Min and their friends. "Merry Christmas!" they called, and soon everyone was hugging and laughing and talking.

Still, for one awful moment, Ruby was afraid that they had made a terrible, terrible mistake. She and Olivia and Flora hadn't thought about what would happen when Mae saw Nikki's friends rush onto the porch. Would she suspect that Mr. Willet wasn't the real Santa?

But Mae looked from the visitors to Santa Claus with her shining face and said, "So they're your helpers this year?"

"That's right," said Mr. Willet.

"Nikki! Flora and Ruby and Olivia are Santa's helpers!" exclaimed Mae.

"Your map was very good," Ruby said to her, "but Santa called us for some more directions."

"Mommy, can we open the presents now?" asked Mae, giving a little skip. "Please?"

"I think we should save them for tomorrow, don't you?" replied Mrs. Sherman.

"One then, please?" said Mae. "I can't wait until tomorrow for everything." She paused. "That's just asking too much."

Mr. Willet choked back a laugh, and Mrs. Sherman smiled. "One present," she said. "But let's all go inside. It's freezing out here."

Ruby didn't know it, but Nikki's house had never seen so many visitors before. In no time, the presents had been carried inside, and the food had been put away in the kitchen, and everyone gathered in the living room.

Mae treated Mr. Willet like royalty. "Have a cookie," she said. "Do you want some milk? No, you probably get a lot of milk." She led him to an armchair and made him sit down. "How long can you stay?" she asked. "I know you have a lot more deliveries to make."

"This is my busiest night of the year, as you know," said Mr. Willet, "but I can stay for a little visit."

"Oh, goody," said Mae, and she climbed into his lap.

Ruby was standing with Flora and Olivia by the Shermans' tree, looking at the decorations. Nikki joined them. She fingered a papier-mâché star and said shyly, "I made this in third grade."

"I made one just like it when I was in third grade!" said Olivia. "Only I didn't know you then."

"This time last year I didn't know *any* of you," said Nikki.

"I didn't have any best friends," said Olivia.

"And Flora and I still lived in our old town," said Ruby.

"I can't believe you guys did this," said Nikki. "I really can't. Nothing like this has ever happened to us before."

"Mommy!" called Mae suddenly. "You said I could open one present. Could I open it now? *Please?* I'm going to explode."

"My goodness, we can't have that," said Mr. Willet. "Which present would you like to open?"

Everyone looked at Mae, waiting for her answer. "You choose, Santa," she said to Mr. Willet.

Mr. Willet, pretending to make a serious decision, laid one finger beside his nose, and Mae gasped. "Don't nod!" she cried. "Please don't nod, or up the chimney you'll rise."

Mr. Willet smiled. "I won't leave yet," he assured her. He surveyed the stack of presents that were for Mae and, after much apparent thinking and consideration, selected one. (Ruby grinned at Flora; Mr. Willet had no idea what was in any of the packages.)

Mac plopped down on the floor. The present was large, wrapped in candy cane paper and tied with green ribbon. Before untying the bow, Mae regarded the gift with awe. Then she opened it carefully. "The piano!" she shrieked. "Mommy, it's the piano! And it's exactly the one I was hoping for! Oh, thank you, Santa! Thank you, thank you, thank you!"

Mae plinked at the keys and Ruby thought she could make out the beginnings of "Jingle Bells."

Min looked at her watch then and said, "Heavenly days, McGee! It's late. We should be on our way."

And the next thing Ruby knew, Nikki had thrown her arms around first her, then Olivia, and finally Flora. "This is the best Christmas ever," she said. "I never expected anything like it. I don't know how you did it, but thank you."

"That's what friends are for," said Ruby.

Everyone began to put on their outdoor clothes then and the room grew quiet. But when all the buttoning and tying and zipping had been accomplished, the house became noisy again.

"I'll call you tomorrow," Nikki said to her friends.

"Thank you for everything," said Mrs. Sherman warmly.

"Thank you, Santa," said Tobias, grinning. He shook Mr. Willet's hand, and then he hugged Ruby and Flora and Olivia. "Nikki is lucky to have friends like you," he whispered.

Mr. Willet was the last one to leave, and Mae said suddenly, "Where's your sleigh?"

Ruby turned around in horror and saw Mr. Willet's eyes widen, but he said nonchalantly, "It's down at the end of your lane. I was having some landing problems. Merry Christmas, Mae! I'll be back next year. Ho! Ho! Ho!"

The last thing Ruby heard before the Shermans' door closed was Mae calling, "I love you, Santa!"

Ruby trudged down the snowy lane again. The clouds had cleared and the stars were out. A full moon, too. Ruby felt that must mean something special — a full moon on Christmas Eve — and even with the fake Santa walking along ahead of her, she swept her eyes back and forth across the night sky. What if, just what if, she saw the real Santa's sleigh up there, silhouetted against the great shining moon? She glanced at her sister and knew that Flora was thinking the exact same thing. Because after all, it was Christmas Eve, and on Christmas Eve anything might happen.

CHAPTER 17

The Night Before Christmas

"I'm starving!" Flora exclaimed as she and Min and Ruby opened the door to the Row House.

"Then it's a good thing we're just about to have our Christmas Eve dinner," said Min. "My, we'll be eating late tonight."

"What do you have for Christmas Eve dinner?" asked Ruby, sounding suspicious. "Dad always made oyster stew because he said that's what *his* father used to have on Christmas Eve. But Flora and I don't like oysters. Or anything that used to live in a shell."

"Luckily, Dad never made us eat the oyster stew," added Flora. "He said that on Christmas Eve, people shouldn't have to eat things they don't like."

"We're going to have a smorgasbord," said Min. "Allie!" she called. "We're back!"

"What kind of a smorgasbord?" asked Flora.

"This kind." Min began taking jars and packages and platters out of the refrigerator.

"Oh, look! Teeny bread!" exclaimed Ruby. "I love teeny bread."

"It's fancy," agreed Flora.

"We'll make fancy sandwiches," said Min. "There's roast beef and turkey and all the trimmings."

Dinner was eaten in the kitchen with carols playing softly on the radio. Min and Aunt Allie recalled Christmases when Allie was a little girl.

"I remember one year," said Allie, looking at her nieces, "when I was six and your mother was nine — and I still believed in Santa. I really, truly thought I heard sleigh bells outside and I nearly had a heart attack because I wasn't asleep yet and I thought Santa would skip our house if I was still awake. Of course the next morning our stockings were filled and there were presents under the tree."

"What about the sleigh bells?" asked Ruby.

"It was your mom jingling a set of house keys," said Allie.

Flora smiled. "What else do you remember?"

"I remember the year — I think I was in high school — when Mother had absolutely convinced me that I wasn't going to get this very expensive bicycle I'd been asking for. She kept saying things like, 'You're in Fantasyland, Allie.' But on Christmas morning, there it was."

Min chuckled. "It was harder to surprise you girls when you were older."

"Min? What's your favorite Christmas memory?" asked Flora.

"Laws, that's a tough question. I have so many wonderful memories. One thing I liked a lot, though, was going to church on Christmas Eve. We used to do that when I was little. We went to church every Sunday then, and on holidays, too, and, oh, sitting in that hushed, chilly room with candles burning and the stained glass windows seeming to glow, snow falling sometimes, listening to the minister read the Christmas story from the Bible. That's one of my best memories."

They had finished dinner and Flora said, "On Christmas Eve, we always make hot chocolate and read *The Night Before Christmas.*"

"Then I think that's exactly what we should do now," said Min.

"I'll help you clear the table," said Allie, "but after that, I'm going to head upstairs. I have a little work to do."

"On Christmas *Eve?*" cried Flora, and Ruby said, "You're not going to hang your stocking?"

Aunt Allie was standing at the sink, a stack of plates in her hands. "Oh, you can hang it for me," she said over her shoulder.

"But —" Flora started to say, and then found that

she was so astonished, she couldn't even finish the sentence.

"Can't the work wait a bit?" Min said gently to Allie.

Flora couldn't see her aunt's face, but she had a feeling Allie rolled her eyes before replying (with a sigh), "Okay. Call me when the hot chocolate is ready."

Flora set herself outside the moment. After all, she barely knew her aunt; why should she care if Allie was a supremely rude creature? The most important people in Flora's life at that moment were Ruby and Min, and they were excited about the festivities. Min was bustling around the kitchen, tidying up and humming along to "Good King Wenceslas," and Ruby was setting out mugs and looking for the cocoa powder.

"I'll bet," said Min, "that each of us in this room knows a good secret that will be revealed tomorrow."

"Yup," said Ruby. "I definitely do."

"So do I," said Min.

"Me, too," said Flora, feeling a little wiggle of anticipation. "Lots of them."

When the hot chocolate was ready, Ruby carried it into the living room on Min's Santa Claus tray. Ruby liked the tray a lot, but she couldn't help feeling that it was the *wrong* tray. Last year on Christmas Eve, she and Flora and their mom and dad had sat in their old living room in their old house drinking their old brand of hot chocolate. Ruby had had the job of carrying the tray of hot chocolate to the living room. The tray they always used on Christmas Eve was square and red and in the middle said COOKIES FOR SANTA, and this was the correct and proper tray.

Ruby gave herself a short lecture. The Santa face tray is very nice, she said. Think how lucky you are. Lots of kids have no tree, no presents, no Christmas, not even a Santa face tray.

But she still missed the old tray just a little.

Soon, though, when Ruby and Flora and Min and Aunt Allie were sitting in the living room, each holding a cup of hot chocolate, a fire crackling in the hearth, King Comma and Daisy Dear on hand to see what would happen next, Ruby found that she could focus on right now instead of a year ago. Look ahead, she reminded herself, not back.

For a few moments, the living room was very, very quiet. Ruby listened to the fire and to Daisy Dear, who began to snore, and she thought she could hear distant church bells. Finally, Min said, "Well, I never. Christmas Eve and nobody has anything to say?"

Ruby, despite her lecture, swallowed a large lump in her throat. But she set down her mug and said, "Flora, where's *The Night Before Christmas?* We brought it from home, didn't we?"

"I'll get it," said Flora. "It's in my room, I think."

"Allie, do you know," said Min, "I believe we still have the copy you and Frannie used to read. I'll get that one, too. We'll read from your copy, Ruby, but you and Flora might enjoy looking at the old one."

"Why?" asked Ruby.

"You'll see."

Min disappeared upstairs, and a few minutes later she and Flora returned to the living room, each carrying a copy of *The Night Before Christmas*.

"Who should read?" asked Min.

"That was Ruby's job," said Flora. "Starting when she was in second grade, anyway, and old enough to read the book."

"Did you have a job?" Aunt Allie asked Flora.

"I used to be in charge of writing the note to Santa. When we were too old for that, Mom and Dad gave me another job. I got to play Santa on Christmas Eve."

"Play Santa?" asked Min.

"We were allowed to open one present each after we had hung our stockings, and I chose the presents."

"Ah," said Min.

Ruby found herself brightening at the thought of opening the early presents. She sat back on the couch. Daisy Dear shifted, resting her giant head in Ruby's lap, and didn't seem to mind when Ruby used the top of her head as a resting place for *The Night Before Christmas*.

Ruby drew in her breath and, in her slightly too-loud stage voice, intoned, "'Twas the night before Christmas and all through the house, not a creature was stirring, not even a mouse.'"

Ruby's favorite part of the poem (aside from saying "threw up the sash," which still made her giggle) was, for reasons she couldn't explain, the part about the moon on the breast of the new-fallen snow. Maybe it was because she liked the picture on that page — an image of a tiny, sleeping town, its church steeples and rooftops and streets buried in a blanket of snow. The town, she realized, could be Camden Falls.

Ruby closed the book while she was still reciting the last lines of the story (to indicate that in actuality she had memorized the entire poem and didn't need the book at all), and laid it beside her on the couch. "'. . . a merry Christmas to all, and to all a good night,'" she said in her Alice Kendall voice.

"That was lovely, Ruby," said Min.

"You're a very good reader," said Aunt Allie approvingly.

"Would you girls like to see your mother's old copy of the story?" asked Min. She handed the book to Flora, who scooted next to Ruby on the couch. They opened the book and looked at the first page, then turned to the second page. They turned several more pages and Ruby finally exclaimed, "Someone drew glasses on every single person in the book!"

"And the mice and all the reindeer!" cried Flora. "Every living creature."

From her spot in an armchair, Aunt Allie burst out laughing. "Oh, Mother! I'd forgotten about that!"

"Did *you* draw the glasses?" asked Flora in amazement.

"Your mother and I both did. We did it together one Christmas Eve when we got impatient waiting to hang our stockings. We thought we were being awfully funny."

Ruby heard a catch in her aunt's voice and looked up from the book.

"Sorry," said Allie.

"No reason to be sorry," said Min, and Ruby heard a catch in her grandmother's voice, too.

Ruby looked from Min to her aunt and back and understood that she and Flora were not the only ones missing people on this frosty Christmas Eve. She clasped Flora's hand briefly, and then Min said to Flora, "All right, Santa Claus. Choose a present for each of us, and then it will be time to hang stockings and go to bed. It's getting late, and you girls had a big day."

Flora knelt by the Christmas tree. "Hmm," she said, and made a great show of examining packages and reading tags.

"Just choose them!" Ruby finally yelped from the couch. "I can't wait any longer!"

Flora chose four small gifts and handed them out.

Min exclaimed over a pin from Aunt Allie. "You'd think I'd get too old for new jewelry," she said, "but I never do."

Aunt Allie opened a box containing a rubber stamp from Flora. "See? It's a computer," said Flora. "You can stamp it on your envelopes and everyone will know you're a writer."

"Very thoughtful," said Aunt Allie.

Flora's gift was from Min, a copy of *Half Magic*, which Flora had been wanting to read.

And Ruby's gift was a pair of mittens that Min had knitted.

"When did you make them?" asked Ruby. "I never saw you working on them. Very sneaky. Thank you, Min!"

The stockings were hung then, and moments later, Ruby and Flora were banished to their bedrooms.

"Good night!" they called. "See you on Christmas morning!"

CHAPTER 18

Merry Christmas!

Christmas Eve had been a long and busy day, and Flora had little difficulty falling asleep that night. She remembered long-ago Christmases when she had lain awake for hours listening for the pawing of reindeer hooves on the roof, or sleigh runners crunching to a halt in the snow by the chimney. And she remembered the previous Christmas when she had wished so hard for her very own sewing machine (a gift she wasn't certain her parents would deem her old enough to warrant) that she had stared wide-eyed about her room until after midnight. But on this Christmas Eve, she nestled under her blankets, King Comma curling up against her chest, and felt as though she had just barely drifted off when she was awakened by Ruby jumping up and down at the foot of her bed, exclaiming softly, "It's Christmas, Flora! It's Christmas morning! Get up!"

"No," mumbled Flora. "It's the middle of the night. Go back to bed before you wake Min."

"It is *not* the middle of the night" Ruby replied indignantly. "It's almost six-thirty. Come on — get *up*. Please?"

Flora rolled over and checked her clock. "Ruby," she said, "I think you'd better wait until seven at least."

"Oh, I can't, I can't," Ruby wailed, and then said again, "It's Christmas!"

"Get in bed with me," said Flora. "King Comma is here, too. You can wait with us."

Flora tried to go back to sleep, but Ruby wriggled and squirmed and tossed so mightily that Flora nearly fell out of bed, and King gave a disdainful meow and emerged, looking very put out, from under the covers, the sheet trailing behind him like a veil. At five minutes to seven, when Ruby kicked Flora in the knee, Flora finally said, "Okay. Go wake up Min and Aunt Allie."

"I'll wake up Min, but not Aunt Allie," said Ruby, and she dashed down the hall, calling, "Min! Min! Merry Christmas!"

Flora yawned and stretched and saw the hall light blink on. She looked out her window. Lights were glowing softly in the houses across the street. Camden Falls was rising early this morning.

"I can't wait another minute!" Flora heard Ruby say from the hallway. "Please can we get up now?"

"I think we're already up," Min replied.

Flora slipped into the hall. "Merry Christmas, Min," she said.

"Good lord in heaven, what time is it?" That was Aunt Allie, and everyone turned to watch her progress down the stairs from the third floor.

"Seven o'clock on the dot!" said Ruby, which wasn't quite true, but Aunt Allie looked far too sleepy to care.

Min tied the sash of her bathrobe around her ample waist and patted her hair. "Look at me. I'm a fright," she said. "But no matter. Now, everyone wait here while I light the fire."

"*Wait?!*" wailed Ruby.

"Could you start the coffee, too?" said Aunt Allie, who had lowered herself onto the bottom step.

"Oh, *oh*." Ruby groaned dramatically, but she sat next to Allie, and Flora sat next to her, and they all waited silently.

Five agonizing minutes later, Flora heard crackling. The smell of wood smoke drifted up the stairs. Five more minutes and she could smell coffee.

"Okay!" Ruby shouted from her place on the step. "I smell coffee and the fire! Can we come down now?"

"You can come," said Min.

Ruby flew down the stairs, Flora behind her, Aunt Allie, moving at a slower pace, behind Flora.

Ruby made a dash for the stockings, but Flora stopped suddenly as she entered the living room. This moment, this perfect Christmas moment, happened only once each year. It was the few seconds in which she could glimpse the stuffed stockings hanging from the mantel, a fire in the hearth, the shining tree surrounded by wrapped gifts; the few seconds before the first bit of wrapping paper was removed and Christmas began to unravel. This wasn't her old house, this wasn't her old living room or fireplace, and these weren't her familiar decorations. But Flora found the scene as heart-stopping as always, and she paused to look, just look — and then Ruby grabbed her stocking and dumped it on the floor.

"Oh!" Ruby cried. "A stuffed reindeer! A candy cane! A light-up pen! Ooh, chocolate! And marzipan! Thank you!"

She pawed through her bounty while Flora regarded her stocking, then reverently released it from its hook and carried it to the couch. She admired it for several more seconds before withdrawing the first gift and unwrapping it slowly. A bar of soap in vibrant pink and green.

"That's from Daisy," Min said to Flora. "She did her own shopping this year."

Flora giggled. "Good choice, Daisy. Thank you."

"Look! A lottery ticket!" exclaimed Aunt Allie. "Thank you, Mother."

"A chocolate Santa," said Min.

"A magic trick," said Ruby.

"Rubber stamps!" cried Flora.

"Earrings," said Aunt Allie.

"Don't forget the stockings for King Comma and Daisy Dear," said Flora.

King had followed everyone into the living room and had curled up in front of the fire, sound asleep again, before he'd even eaten his breakfast. But Daisy was seated directly beneath her stocking, staring at it pointedly.

"Do you smell something good in there?" Min asked her.

Daisy's tail thumped the floor lustily.

"Can I open her presents?" asked Ruby. "I'm done with my stocking."

"You're *done*?" said Flora. "Already?" Her own stocking, and Min's and Aunt Allie's, were still half stuffed.

"Done!" cried Ruby. She inserted a marzipan pig in her mouth and reached for Daisy's stocking. "What did you get from Santa, Daisy Dear?" she said.

Daisy got a squeaky toy in the shape of a candy cane, a rawhide bone, a package of Greenies treats, and, much to Flora's disgust, a brand-new hoof for gnawing on. It was the hoof that Daisy had smelled, and she snuffled at Ruby's hand as she unwrapped it.

"Pew! Those hoof things sti —" Flora started to say. She paused. "They really smell."

"But Daisy really loves them," said Ruby. "And on Christmas, everybody gets treats. Can she have it right now, Min?"

"She may," said Min, and Daisy retreated to the hearth rug, where she lay down, one hind leg delicately outstretched, the revolting hoof anchored between her front paws, and chewed with great concentration.

"Merry Christmas, Daisy!" said Ruby.

Aunt Allie claimed that she needed her coffee then in order to get the cobwebs out of her head, so Min went into the kitchen. When she returned, carrying two mugs, Ruby said, "Can I give you all my best present right now?" she said. "It's for everybody together, and I can't wait one single second longer to give it to you. Here. Sit on the couch," said Ruby. And she added, "This is my best secret of the day."

Flora sat between Min and Aunt Allie, coffee sloshing in their mugs, since Ruby had seated them rather forcibly. Then Ruby disappeared from the living room for a moment. When she returned, she stood before them in her nightgown, saying, "My gift to you is a song. I hope you like it. Merry Christmas."

Ruby clasped her hands together, closed her eyes as she sometimes did before a musical performance, and began to sing in her clear, steady voice. *"Angels we have heard on high, sweetly singing o'er the plains."* By the time she had reached the third line, Min was sniffling, and Aunt Allie put her hand to her heart.

"Oh, my. That was lovely, Ruby," said Min, her voice catching, when Ruby had sung the last *"Gloria in excelsis Deo."*

"A wonderful gift," agreed Aunt Allie. "You have a beautiful voice, Ruby."

And Flora said, "How did you keep that a secret? That was a good one, Ruby. We never even heard you rehearsing."

Ruby grinned and blushed slightly. "I have other presents for you," she said, "but that was the main one."

Min said it was time to stop and have breakfast, which caused Ruby to stare dolefully at the packages under the tree, but Min added that she had made a special Christmas coffee cake, so everyone went happily into the dining room. Later, they gathered around the tree again, and now it was Flora who couldn't wait to hand out her presents.

"The special ones," she said.

The special gifts were the ones Flora had made: a sachet in rich purples and reds for Aunt Allie, a striped hat for Ruby, and a box of stationery for Min.

"You made this?" exclaimed Min when she opened the box.

Flora nodded. "Using rubber stamps, gold ink, and the embosser — which I always remembered to unplug," she added hastily.

"Oh, my goodness, this is lovely. Everything is lovely."

After that, Min played Santa Claus, and the morning passed slowly and quickly at the same time. When all the gifts had been opened, Flora had new clothes (some made by Min), a scrapbook from Mary Woolsey (the pages blank, but the cover exquisitely embroidered by Mary), a pile of books, new art supplies, and everything she would need to knit a hat and matching mittens. This last gift had come from Aunt Allie, who must have rethought her savings account idea. Flora was certain Min had helped her choose the items, but she didn't care. And when she thanked her aunt, she gave her a hug.

"Saints preserve us," said Min, looking at the stew of torn paper and ribbon bits and boxes on the floor. "Time to clean up a bit. Mr. Pennington is coming over for lunch, you know."

By the time he arrived, Flora and her family had showered and dressed (mostly in new clothes), and they greeted him fresh-faced at the door. More presents were exchanged, and in the afternoon, Olivia came over to see Flora's and Ruby's presents, and then they went to Olivia's to see hers. Lacey came over later, then Ruby went to Lacey's, and before Flora knew it, darkness had fallen, and the day was nearly over.

Supper that night was the leftovers from Christmas Eve dinner. Flora was chewing the last bite of a teeny roast beef sandwich when the phone rang. Ruby made a dash for it and answered, saying, "Merry Christmas! This is Ruby!" She listened for a moment, then grinned and said, "Flora, it's Nikki. Pick up the other phone."

"Hi, you guys," said Nikki. "We had the *best* day."

"So did we," said Flora.

"I was wondering — would you and Olivia like to come over tomorrow? You know, just to see everything. Mae's having so much fun with all the presents. And Tobias made a jewelry box for me, and we both made a toy chest for Mae. And I don't know. Do you want to come over?"

Flora drew in her breath. Apart from the previous night's visit, she and Ruby and Olivia had never once been to Nikki's house, and she had been their friend since the summer.

"Yes!" said Flora. "Yes! We'll be there."

And that was how Flora's first Christmas in Camden Falls drew to a close. That night, she slept a deep and satisfied sleep with King Comma.

CHAPTER 19

Mrs. Grindle's News

Olivia, too, was fully satisfied with Christmas. She was sorry it was over, of course, and that she'd have to wait an entire year for it to come again, but she had to admit that the holiday, which her parents described as the reduced-fat version, had been one of the best ever. Among the remarkable homemade gifts she received was a set of bookends painted with glorious butterflies from her father and a scrapbook of the Walters' summer carefully decorated by her mother. Henry gave her a coupon worth one cleaning out of Olivia's bedroom, and Jack (with the help of Flora, Olivia suspected) had made her a beaded ring. There were other gifts, too, including a promise from her father to take her to the zoo in Barrington, where a butterfly garden was to open in the spring. So all in all, despite her parents' altered finances, it was a fine holiday (although Olivia realized that the finest aspect was knowing that her family aimed to stay in Camden Falls).

The week between Christmas and New Year's Eve was a busy one for Olivia. On Wednesday, the day after Christmas, she and Ruby and Flora visited Nikki at her house.

"I'm just a teensy bit nervous," Olivia whispered after Flora and Ruby's aunt had dropped them off at the Shermans'.

"Me, too," said Flora.

"Why?" asked Ruby. "Nikki's father isn't here."

"What if he comes back?"

"He didn't come back for Christmas," Ruby pointed out. "Why would he come back now?"

"Ruby's right. He won't come back," said Olivia with more confidence than she felt.

The girls stood uncertainly in a line on Nikki's front stoop.

"The house looks different now than it did on Christmas Eve," said Flora.

"Everything was magic on Christmas Eve," said Olivia.

The door was flung open then, and Nikki, grinning, exclaimed, "Are you going to stand there all morning?"

Mae appeared behind her. "Hi!" she cried. "Oh, goody, you can see what Santa brought! You only saw the piano. But he brought books, too, and a doll and clothes for her. I named the doll Chesapeake," she added. "Oh, and Nikki and Tobias made a chest for my toys. Come in. You have to see everything." Mae grabbed Olivia and Flora and hauled them through the doorway. "Come on, Ruby," she called over her shoulder. "Come with us."

Olivia looked around the living room, which seemed somewhat less festive than it had when Santa Claus was standing in the middle of it.

"Hi, girls," said Mrs. Sherman, wiping her hands on a paper towel and turning off the kitchen light before she joined them.

Olivia regarded Nikki's mother. She saw hard lines around her mouth, and she noted that her hair had probably been dyed, given the color of the roots (black) versus the rest of the hair (reddish brown). Olivia's own mother was not partial to dyed hair, but Olivia refrained from drawing any conclusions based on the hair alone.

"Hi," chorused Olivia, Flora, and Ruby.

For a moment after that, no one seemed to know what to say. Flora gazed out the window, and Ruby watched Mae dress Chesapeake. Luckily, Paw-Paw entered the room then. Olivia knelt on the floor to pat him.

"He likes to be scratched behind his ears," said Nikki. So Olivia scratched his ears, and Paw-Paw squinted his eyes in rapture and finally extended his paw.

Mae, glancing at him, said, "That's how he got his name."

"Mom, we're going to go to my room for a while," said Nikki, standing.

"Me, too! I'm going with them," announced Mae.

"Nope," said Mrs. Sherman gently. "You're going to help me in the kitchen. We'll make lunch. Let Nikki have the room to herself."

Olivia followed the others up a dim staircase and into the small bedroom Nikki shared with Mae.

"This is my room," said Nikki. "I know it isn't anything like your rooms, but —"

"Oh, no, it's wonderful!" cried Flora. "I've tried to picture it, and just like I imagined, you put some of your artwork on the walls."

"And, um," said Ruby, casting about for something to add, "you sure have a colorful bedspread."

"The most important thing about your room," said Olivia, "is that it's yours. Now we know another little piece of you — and when I talk to you on the phone, I'll be able to imagine you sitting in that chair by that window in this room."

The four girls crowded onto Nikki's bed.

"So," said Nikki, "tell me about your Christmases."

And they did. Nikki showed off the jewelry box and the toy chest, both already carefully placed in the bedroom. Then Olivia, her mind on her own family's troubles, said, "Nikki? Can I ask you something?"

"Sure."

"And if it's too personal, just say so. You don't have to answer."

"Okay."

"Well, I've been wondering — how are you doing since your father left? I mean, you know, with money and everything?"

Olivia saw the slightest frown crease Nikki's forehead, but then it disappeared, and Nikki replied, "We're all right, but just barely. We had a little bit of money before Dad left. Now it's gone, though, and Dad hasn't sent any money, of course, so Mom needs to find a full-time job. She's already started looking for one, but, well, it's going to be hard to find one that pays enough to support four people. And Mae will need day care when she's not in school. That's another expense. Also," said Nikki, and she began to pick at the edge of her bedspread, "I never told you this, but you probably heard it, you know, around. My mom is an alcoholic. But the good thing is that she hasn't had one single drink since my father left. She says she plans to keep it that way, and I believe her. She also said it won't be easy. I believe that, too."

Olivia was just going to say that she wasn't entirely clear what an alcoholic was, when she heard a robust knock at the door and Mae yelled, "Lunch is ready! Come and get it!"

All during the rest of her visit to Nikki's house,

Olivia pondered the word "alcoholic," and at lunchtime, she glanced discreetly at Mrs. Sherman for clues. She knew it had something to do with drinking alcoholic beverages, of course, but except for the unfortunately dyed hair, Olivia didn't see many differences between Mrs. Sherman and her own mother. Mrs. Sherman smiled often. She spoke gently to Mae, who tended to be loud and energetic. She joined the girls for lunch and asked them about school and their families, and she didn't refrain from asking Ruby and Flora about the accident and about how they were adjusting to Camden Falls. Later, when Nikki said she wanted to take Paw-Paw on a walk and show her friends the yard and the countryside (which Olivia appreciated, being a town girl with a small backyard), Mrs. Sherman again occupied Mae, even when Mae threw a small tantrum, claiming that she was one of the big girls and ought to be allowed to go along.

The day passed comfortably, and when Allie returned to pick up Olivia and Flora and Ruby, the girls were reluctant to leave.

"But I'll see you tomorrow," said Nikki. "I'll come to the store, okay?"

And she did. In fact, Nikki was sitting in Needle and Thread with Olivia, Flora, and Ruby late the next afternoon when Olivia's world came crashing down once again (as Olivia would say in later retellings of the story). Darkness had already fallen and Nikki was waiting for Tobias to pick her up. She and Ruby were sitting together on one of the chat-and-stitch couches, using colored pencils to design outfits they would like to wear, and Olivia and Flora were sitting on the other couch reading *Half Magic* together, which was a bit difficult since Olivia was a faster reader than Flora. (Olivia was a faster reader than most people.) But Olivia didn't mind. Every time she finished a page before Flora did, she would simply lean back and look around the store and think how cozy it was and how wonderful her life was, while she waited for Flora to catch up.

She was doing just that when the bell over the door rang and in walked her mother from another day at Stuff 'n' Nonsense.

"What's wrong?" asked Olivia immediately.

Her mother gave her a tired smile. "Not much, really."

"Something happened, though, didn't it?"

"Yes, but it's a good thing for Mrs. Grindle."

Min thanked the last customer of the day, closed the door behind him, and put the CLOSED sign in the window. She and Gigi perched on one of the couches.

Olivia, who had been so happy just moments earlier, now felt the familiar sinking in her stomach.

"What is it?" asked Gigi.

"Mrs. Grindle has decided not to sell Stuff 'n' Nonsense after all."

"What? Why?" cried Olivia.

"She didn't really want to sell the store in the first place," her mother answered.

"But she said it was hard to keep it going!" Olivia protested.

"I know. She had some time to think things over, though, and she's going to take some of our suggestions. She's going to hire more help, and she decided to close the store one more day each week."

"Well, that's wonderful," said Min. "I mean for Gina. Selling the store would have been an enormous change for her."

"But what about *us*?" said Olivia, who was close to tears.

Nikki, Flora, and Ruby looked puzzled. Then Flora said, "Your parents will find another place."

"They already *had* found another place," said Olivia. "Two, actually. And they were far away and we were going to have to *move*!"

"What?!" cried Ruby, and she made a great display of clapping her hand to her face.

But Mrs. Walter only said mildly, "Girls, nothing was definite."

"It was definite enough!" said Olivia. "You talked to us about leaving Camden Falls and —"

Mrs. Walter sat down next to Olivia. She put her arm around her shoulders. "But it *wasn't* definite, not entirely, and we put everything on hold when we thought we were going to buy Stuff 'n' Nonsense. I know you don't want to move, Olivia, but can you please not jump to conclusions? Let's just see how things play out."

Olivia mumbled that this was easy for her mother to say, and then she burst into tears and ran into the storeroom, slamming the door behind her.

For a few moments, Olivia leaned against a stack of packing cartons, trying to control her breathing and put a stop to her sobs. From the other side of the closed door she heard a jumble of voices and then her mother saying softly, "No, leave her alone. Let her work this out."

Olivia slid to the floor. She dried her eyes. And then, for no reason she could explain, her mind jumped to the evening Mrs. Grindle had sat, exhausted, on the couch at Needle and Thread and said how tired she was. After that, thought Olivia, she had said something else, something about Ma Grand-mère. What was it? Olivia closed her eyes and concentrated. Ellen and Carol had told Mrs. Grindle that their business was beginning to feel like a burden. A burden and not a pleasure.

Olivia wondered whether this was still true. And she pictured Ma Grand-mère with its lovely professional kitchen. Then she tiptoed to the back door of Needle and Thread, slipped outside, and made her way up the block.

CHAPTER 20

The End of the Year

On the Sunday after Christmas, Nikki was standing in her mother's bedroom, studying herself before the full-length mirror. Thin, but not too thin, she thought, and she realized she was starting to fill out just a little in a few key places. She was scrutinizing her hair (straight and plain brown) when she heard a car turn onto the lane to her house. Tobias and her mother were home, so who had arrived? Mrs. DuVane? If so, Nikki planned to thank her profusely for the clothing and art supplies Mrs. DuVane had given her for Christmas.

Nikki abandoned the mirror and crossed the room to the window. She peered down and saw a truck pull to a stop at the end of the drive. And she let out a shriek.

"Mom! Mom!" she called. She thundered down the stairs. "Mom!"

Mrs. Sherman hurried out of the kitchen. "Nikki? What's wrong, honey? What is it?"

"Dad's back! I swear it. He's back. He's getting out of the truck right now. I just saw him from the window."

Tobias rose from the couch, where he'd been watching a football game on TV. He strode to the front door and flung it open, surprising Mr. Sherman, who already had his hand on the knob and nearly fell inside.

"What are you doing here?" asked Tobias.

"Well, that's a nice greeting," Mr. Sherman replied. He looked at his wife, at Nikki, at Tobias, all standing warily in the living room. Mae was there, too, dressing Chesapeake. After a moment, she got to her feet and said, "Hi, Daddy."

"Don't you have a hug for your dad?" said Mr. Sherman.

Mae glanced sideways at Nikki, then stepped forward and put her arms stiffly around her father's waist. He patted her head.

"Nice coming home for Christmas," said Tobias.

"I never said I'd be back for Christmas."

"Nice sending us money while you were away. Nice keeping your 'promises.'"

"Tobias," said Mrs. Sherman.

"Well, he can't just walk in here like nothing happened."

"Look, I came back. For a surprise visit. What more do you want?" said Mr. Sherman.

"Lots of things. For starters, how about an explana-
tion —" said Tobias.

"Tobias, this is between your father and me," Mrs.
Sherman interrupted.

"No, it's not. What *he* does" (Tobias stuck his thumb
in the direction of Mr. Sherman) "affects all of us."

Nikki looked at her father, still standing in the
doorway; at her mother, backing toward the kitchen; at
Mae, following her mother; at Tobias, who had crossed
his arms and was standing opposite Mr. Sherman. And
then she looked behind Tobias and saw Paw-Paw in the
living room. Paw-Paw had been asleep on the couch
next to Tobias. Ordinarily, when someone came to the
door, Paw-Paw greeted the visitor with noisy and
affronted barking. But he had remained silent during
Mr. Sherman's entrance, and now Nikki watched him
try to slink unnoticed into the kitchen.

Mr. Sherman frowned. "What's that?" he said
sharply. "*What* is *that*, and why is it in the house?" He
took a step forward.

Mae turned to see Paw-Paw, tail between his legs,
eyes averted from Mr. Sherman as he inched forward.
She opened her mouth, then closed it.

"*That* is our dog," said Tobias.

"Yeah, and he's a boy, not an it," said Mae.

Mr. Sherman glared around at his family. "What
have I said — what have I *always said* — about having
filth like that in the house?" In a flash, so quickly that

even Tobias couldn't stop him, Mr. Sherman lunged into the living room, grabbed Paw-Paw by one leg, and yanked him toward the door.

Paw-Paw let out a yelp of pain and surprise, and Mae screamed.

"Dad! Don't!" cried Nikki. "Let him go! Please let him go! I'll take him outside. I'll — I'll get rid of him." Nikki reached for Paw-Paw, and Mr. Sherman let go of him and grabbed Nikki instead.

Later, when Nikki tried to tell her friends what had happened, she found that she couldn't quite remember the next few moments. All she knew was that eventually she was sitting on the floor, holding a struggling Paw-Paw, and Tobias had tackled her father. He was straddling him like a cop on TV, and Nikki realized how big Tobias had gotten. He wrestled Mr. Sherman's arms behind his back.

Mae was still screaming and Paw-Paw was whimpering, and when Tobias let go of one of his father's hands and took hold of his hair instead, jerking his head back, Mrs. Sherman started to scream, too.

"Tobias! Get off him!"

"No!" Tobias slammed his father's forehead onto the floor. "He's going to hurt Nikki. He's going to hurt Paw-Paw. He'll hurt all of us."

"Let . . . me . . . go," said Mr. Sherman, gasping, and Nikki could see blood on his face.

"No," said Tobias again.

"I won't hurt anyone."

"No."

"Howie, you have to leave," Mrs. Sherman said to her husband.

Tobias loosened his grip on his father's hair.

"If I leave now," sputtered Mr. Sherman, and Nikki realized she could see blood oozing from his mouth, too, "I won't come back."

"Good," said Tobias.

Mr. Sherman coughed. "I mean it."

"Good."

To Nikki's surprise, that was the last word that was spoken for more than a minute. In silence, Tobias slid off his father and hauled him to his feet. In silence, Mr. Sherman looked around at his family. (Nikki couldn't read anything in the look, anything at all.) In silence, Mrs. Sherman held the front door open and Tobias shoved his father toward it. And in silence, Mrs. Sherman watched her husband stagger to his truck, climb inside, and drive away. Only when he had reached the end of their lane and turned onto the road did Mrs. Sherman close the door. And then everybody began to cry, even Tobias.

Nikki loosened her hold on Paw-Paw and watched him walk around the room. He was limping, but not badly, and Nikki thought he would be okay. Then she and her mother and Mae huddled together on the couch, while Tobias stalked outside. "I'm going for a walk," he called, and slammed the door behind him.

"Is Daddy really gone forever?" asked Mae.

"Yes, I think so," said Mrs. Sherman.

"Okay," said Mae. "Then I erase him from my mind." She slid off the couch and returned to Chesapeake.

Nikki leaned against her mother, breathing heavily.

Nikki was glad her father had chosen to return on Sunday, because if he had come back on Monday, she didn't think she would have been able to go to the New Year's Eve party at Flora and Ruby's. It was her first-ever slumber party and she didn't want to ruin it, so she was glad to awaken on the day after the awful incident and find that she felt somewhat better. And she was looking forward to the distraction of the party.

Tobias drove her into town that evening. "You're going to stay at home with Mom and Mae tonight, aren't you?" asked Nikki as he turned left at Dutch Haus, then right onto Aiken Avenue.

"Yup."

"Okay," said Nikki. "It's the fourth one," she added as they reached the Row Houses. "Right there."

"Call me tomorrow," said Tobias. "I'll come pick you up."

"Thanks," said Nikki.

Tobias drove off and Nikki felt butterflies in her

stomach, but they disappeared when the busy evening got under way. First there was pizza for supper, which Min insisted on serving the girls in the dining room on her fancy china. "Just for fun," she said, and Nikki, Flora, Olivia, and Ruby pretended they were wealthy and stylish women.

"Like from old movies," said Ruby. "Those ladies who ate with their pinkies up and little dogs asleep in their laps."

After that, they gathered around the TV to watch *Freaky Friday*, and later, they spread their sleeping bags out in Flora's room, Nikki having borrowed a spare from Olivia.

"You know what we should do now?" said Olivia. "You know how on New Year's Eve everyone looks ahead to the next year and makes resolutions? Well, I think instead we should look back over last year and talk about all the stuff that's happened. This has been kind of an amazing year for all of us."

"A year of changes," said Nikki.

"Both good and bad," added Flora.

Ruby stood up on Flora's bed, tilted her face to the ceiling, closed her eyes, waved her hands through the air, and said in a strangely accented voice, "I am ze genie from ze magic lamp. I cast each of us into ze past. One year past! Go back, go back in time to last New Year's Eve, and speak of your life zen. GO!" She opened her eyes and pointed to Olivia. "You in ze blue shirt. You start."

Olivia, trying not to giggle, said, "Well, one year ago, everything was normal. I mean, it seemed normal because it was what I'd always known. Ruby, sit down, okay? I can't do this while you're standing on the bed with that look on your face."

Ruby sat on Flora's bed with a plop.

"Thank you," said Olivia. "Anyway, what I mean is, Dad had his job, the job he'd always had, and we never had to worry about money, which was good. But I barely knew you guys and I didn't have any really close friends. That was bad. At school, I felt like I never belonged. So that was how things were last New Year's Eve. And then in June, you guys moved here," Olivia said to Flora and Ruby, "and suddenly I had real friends right next door! It was like a dream come true. And then, by the end of the summer, we were friends with you, too, Nikki, and for the first time in my life I had an actual *group* of friends.

"But of course by then, Dad had lost his job," Olivia continued. "Another bad thing. But the very worst thing of all was thinking that we might move and I'd have to leave my friends behind.

"So now it's one year later, and I have you guys, and" (Olivia broke into a grin, because she had secretly been waiting all evening for this moment) "Mom and Dad are going to buy Ma Grand-mère."

"What?" cried Nikki, Flora, and Ruby. And Ruby added, "Seriously?"

"Seriously," said Olivia. She told her friends about the idea she'd gotten in Needle and Thread. "So I talked to Carol and Ellen," she went on, "and the next thing I knew, Carol and Ellen were talking to my parents, and now everybody's happy. Carol and Ellen want to move to California, and Mom and Dad are going to buy the store. It's much better for them than Stuff 'n' Nonsense anyway.

"The store will be theirs by the spring. We're going to put up a new sign. Sincerely Yours. Mom is going to make her candy and cookies and things and sell them, and she and Dad will also make baskets like the ones we gave out at Christmas. But they'll be baskets for all occasions — birthdays, baby showers, graduations, holidays, anything. People can come to the store and select the things for the baskets, or we can choose for them. Won't that be cool?" Olivia stopped speaking and looked around at her friends.

"Wow," said Flora.

"That's amazing," said Nikki.

Ruby sprang to her feet and yelped, "Wa-hoo! You get to stay here!"

"Okay, someone else take a turn," said Olivia.

"After that?" said Flora. "I never heard so much news."

"But we all have to say something," replied Olivia.

Ruby glanced at her sister. "I guess we can go together."

"You've been through the most changes," said Olivia.

"And everything happened because of that one night," said Flora.

"Almost a year ago," added Ruby. "In twelve days it will be one year exactly."

"Let's not talk about the night itself," said Flora. "Everyone knows what happened."

"You know what's weird?" said Ruby. "If it hadn't been for the accident, we probably wouldn't all be together right now. Flora and I wouldn't have moved here, and Olivia, you might not have spent so much time at Needle and Thread last summer, so Mrs. DuVane probably wouldn't have thought to bring Nikki to the classes, which means that even you and Nikki wouldn't be friends."

Flora's gaze traveled to the window. "We lost our parents, we moved here to live with Min, we met you guys. Sometimes it's hard to believe."

"Even the good things are hard to believe," said Ruby.

"I'd give anything to have Mom and Dad back," said Flora. "No offense, you guys."

Olivia opened her mouth, closed it, then opened it again and said, "Okay, Nikki, your turn."

"Well," said Nikki, and she could feel color rise to her cheeks, "there are two big differences for me between last year and right now. One is having you guys for friends, and the other is that Dad's gone. Except . . . I didn't tell you what happened yesterday." To Nikki's horror, she felt her lower lip tremble.

"Nikki? Are you crying?" asked Flora, and she scooted across the floor to sit next to her.

"No," said Nikki, and she burst into tears. She cried for a long time while Olivia searched for a box of Kleenex and Ruby looked nervous and Flora put her arm around Nikki's shoulders. When Nikki felt that she had control of her voice again, she told her friends what had happened the day before. Every bit of it, from the moment she had heard the truck outside until her father was gone and she was watching Paw-Paw limp around the living room.

"Are you *sure* you're okay?" asked Olivia.

Nikki nodded.

"And are you sure he won't come back?" asked Ruby.

Nikki nodded again. "His pride was hurt." She paused. "I'm also pretty sure he won't send us any money, but he hadn't sent any anyway, so it doesn't make much difference."

The girls sat quietly until Nikki said, "Is this what usually happens at a sleepover?"

Her friends giggled.

"I don't think this has ever happened at a sleep-over," said Olivia. "This is a first."

"Girls?" called Min then, her voice floating up from the living room. "It's almost midnight. Come join us."

So Nikki and her friends changed into their night-gowns and ran down the stairs. They found Min, Aunt Allie, and Mr. Pennington in the living room. Aunt Allie was writing on her laptop, and Min and Mr. Pennington were sitting companionably on the couch, Min embroidering the collar of a baby dress and Mr. Pennington working a crossword puzzle. The television was on and Nikki could see a shot of Times Square in New York City.

"Hey, I just remembered. Look what we have!" exclaimed Ruby. She disappeared for a moment, then returned lugging a shopping bag into the room. She dumped it on the floor. Out fell noisemakers and paper hats and packages of confetti. Ruby passed out the hats and noisemakers, while Flora opened one of the packages.

"Are you sure it's okay to throw the confetti around?" Flora asked Min. "Think of the mess."

"That's why vacuum cleaners were invented," said Min. "Besides, this only happens once a year."

Ten minutes later, when the ball fell in Times Square and Min's clock chimed midnight, everyone shouted and hugged and blew their horns — even Flora and Ruby's aunt, who had only turned off her computer when everyone began chorusing, "Ten, nine, eight . . ."

For a teeny moment, Nikki, looking at her new friends, the silly hats, and the drifting confetti, thought she might cry again. But she bit her lip and drew in a deep breath.

"Open the front door," said Mr. Pennington suddenly.

"Why?" asked Flora.

"You'll see."

Flora opened the door, and from up and down Aiken Avenue came hoots and cheers and cries of "Happy new year!" Nikki could see sparklers fizzing in the darkness.

"Happy new year, Nikki," said Flora.

"Happy new year."

CHAPTER 21

January

If you were to walk along Main Street in the middle of January, you might not know that Camden Falls had recently been dressed for the holidays. Gone are the wreaths and twinkling lights and the tree in the square. Gone are the menorahs, the Nativity scenes, the Santas, the candy canes. In the store windows now are microwaves and Dustbusters, lamps and bedspreads, mittens and snow shovels. Doubletree Sporting Goods is having a sale on skis and ski boots. In the window of Needle and Thread are bolts of batiste and dotted Swiss and soft cottons, and a sign (lettered by Ruby Northrop) reading THINK SPRING!

On this gray and misty afternoon, if you were to turn off Main Street, you might walk the few blocks to Sonny Sutphin's apartment. Stand in the bleak backyard and look through the ground-floor window into the kitchen. There's Sonny, sitting in his wheel-chair, the newspaper spread open in front of him. His finger is sliding down the Help Wanted ads. Sonny doesn't feel very confident — it's been a long time since he held a job — but he does feel determined. "Computer skills necessary," he murmurs. "Nope. . . . Manual labor. Nope. . . . Store clerk." He looks up from the paper. "Store clerk," he repeats. "I could be a store clerk."

Now leave Sonny behind and take a long walk through the countryside to Nikki Sherman's house. If you were to peek in the windows at the end of this raw day, you would see Tobias sitting with Mae in the living room, helping her with her first-grade homework. In the kitchen, Nikki and her mother are preparing supper.

"Mom," says Nikki, "have you heard from Dad?"

"Not a word."

Nikki considers this. "You know," she says finally, "you don't have to look for day care for Mae. When you find a job, I can watch her after school. That will save some money."

"That's a very nice offer, sweetie," says her mother. "But I want you to have your afternoons free to spend time with your friends or do, well, whatever you want to do. You have enough responsibilities as it is."

"Thanks," Nikki replies. "But isn't day care going to be awfully expensive?"

"Not *awfully* expensive. Anyway, I'm the only one

around here who should worry about money. You concentrate on school, okay?"

"Okay," says Nikki, but she's frowning.

Darkness has fallen, but the walk back into town is pleasant enough in the icy air. Linger outside Mary Woolsey's snug house for a few moments. Mary is sitting on the couch with Daphne and Delilah, reading through some more of her mother's papers. She finds a letter from her father to her mother, and she smiles. Letters from her father are scarce. Then Mary glances at the date at the top of the page, and her smile fades. She puts her hand to her mouth. The letter was written in 1935, three years after the fire at the factory. Her father didn't die then, Mary thinks. Her father survived the fire and her mother knew it.

Now make your way to Aiken Avenue. The Row Houses are as naked as Main Street, their holiday finery returned to attics and cellars and garages. At the curb in front of three of the houses lie brittle evergreen trees, waiting to be picked up by the garbage truck. Olivia Walter finds this very sad.

There's Olivia now, sorting through the photos of Camden Falls wildlife that she took the previous year. Some of them are very good and she's thinking about her project for the 350th birthday celebration. And there are Olivia's parents. They're sitting together in the room on the third floor that used to be Mr. Walter's office. Now it is their shared office, and on this evening, they're looking at the architect's plans for the changes to be made in Ma Grand-mère before it becomes Sincerely Yours. They are holding hands, and Mrs. Walter is smiling.

Walk to the far north end of the Row Houses and you'll see the Fongs. It's a quiet evening and they're talking in the kitchen, feeding their dogs and thinking about their own dinner. Mrs. Fong rests her hand on her belly. "Look!" she says to her husband. "I can almost use it as a tray."

Next door, Robby and Mr. Edwards are making pasta. Robby likes to cook with his father. As he stirs the sauce, he says, "I made a decision today." His father looks at him, eyebrows raised. "In school we were talking about our jobs," says Robby.

"The jobs you'll get after you graduate?"

Robby nods. "Yes. And I think Mrs. Grindle is too mean, so I don't want to work at Stuff 'n' Nonsense after all, even if I like the stickers. I want to work at Olivia's store instead."

"Olivia's store?"

"The one her parents are going to open. I could help with the cooking."

"You are a good cook," agrees his father.

Next door, Mr. Pennington's windows are dark. He has gone to the movies with a friend. Jacques dozes in his dog bed and waits for Mr. Pennington to come back.

That's all he ever does when Mr. Pennington isn't at home.

Now walk to the house at the south end of the row. This one belongs to the Morrises, and it's much quieter than usual. The Morris kids have colds, and their parents have made them all stay in bed today. Mr. and Mrs. Morris are running up and down the stairs, fetching coloring books and apple juice and cough medicine, taking temperatures and encouraging noses to be blown. "This happens every single January," says Mrs. Morris.

Next door, Mr. Willet is busy, but he carries out his tasks with a feeling of dread. He's packing up Mrs. Willet's belongings for her trip to Three Oaks, which will take place in four days. His wife repeatedly asks him what he's doing. "Packing for our trip," he replies each time, trying not to let his voice shake. "Okay," she replies. And then a few minutes later, "What is it that you're doing?" She never uses her husband's name because she isn't certain who this man is.

At the Malones' house, Margaret is sitting at the desk in her room. She's trying to study for a test, but she's having trouble concentrating since in the room across the hall Lydia is having a loud phone fight with Brandi, her former friend. Lydia needs new friends, thinks Margaret, and returns to her biology textbook.

The house to the north of the Malones' is the one

belonging to Min and Flora and Ruby and, for the time being, Aunt Allie — whose visit has lasted much longer than anyone expected. Min is in the kitchen taking a chicken out of the oven and thinking how busy and noisy the house is. This time the year before, just days before the accident that took the lives of her older daughter and her son-in-law, Min would come home each evening to a nearly silent house with only Daisy to greet her and would spend quiet, solitary hours before going to bed.

But on this evening a year later, Ruby is in the downstairs hallway, where she has rolled back the rug and is practicing a tap routine, while she sings "On the Good Ship *Lollipop*." And in the living room, Flora is poised in front of Daisy Dear. She has decided to teach Daisy some tricks, starting with one she calls Ballerina. She's holding a treat above Daisy's head and saying over and over, "Ballerina, Daisy. Ballerina." If Daisy will ever stand up on her hind legs and twirl around once, she will get the treat.

Aunt Allie is in her room on the third floor, writing away madly.

Presently, Min calls her family to dinner. When she and Flora and Ruby and Allie are seated around the kitchen table and have been served, Min says, "So, did everyone have a good day?"

"Yes," chorus Ruby and Flora.

And Allie puts her fork down and says, "I've been

doing a lot of soul searching, and I've come to a decision."

Everyone looks at her, and Flora gets a strange feeling in her stomach.

"Oh?" says Min.

"I think I may remain in Camden Falls permanently."

"My stars and garters," says Min, and silence descends on the dining room.

Ann M. Martin

talks about

Main Street

Q: What's the holiday season like where you live? Is it at all like Camden Falls?

A: I live near Woodstock, New York, and the holiday season here is very much like the one in Camden Falls — and that's because I based most of the Camden Falls traditions on Woodstock's. For instance, Woodstock really does have an open house one evening early in December when people come into town to do their shopping, carolers walk up and down Tinker Street (the main street), and the shopkeepers serve goodies. And on Christmas Eve, after a short parade, Santa Claus always makes a fantastic appearance. He's arrived in a helicopter, emerged from the top of a giant candy cane, and, just like in the book, been lowered to earth in a hot air balloon. It's my all-time favorite annual event.

Q: What are some of your favorite Christmas traditions?

A: My favorite traditions are the ones that lead up to Christmas Day. I love decorating my house and the tree. Some of the decorations belonged to my grandmother when she was a little girl, and others are from my childhood. I'm particularly fond of the macaroni chain my nephew made for me when he was in preschool. Also, I like wrapping gifts and sending out cards, and I especially like to make Christmas presents.

Q: Did you sing carols a lot as a kid?

A: I did sing carols a lot. Several times my sister and friends and I went caroling in our neighborhood. Sometimes one or the other of our neighbors would host a Christmas party and we would sing carols then, too. Now, as an adult, I love listening to Christmas music, especially to traditional carols.

Q: This is not the first book you've written that takes place over the holidays. Your last novel, *On Christmas Eve*, took place — well, on Christmas Eve. What is it about the season that keeps inspiring you to write about it? Do you feel you still have other holiday stories to tell?

A: There are many things I like about Christmas, but I

think I'm especially drawn to the magic of the holiday, which is what I tried to convey in *On Christmas Eve*, and to a certain extent in *'Tis the Season*. Given my feelings about Christmas, this is probably not the last holiday story I'll write!

Q: Every year, you send out Christmas cards "starring" your pets. What were some of your favorites?

A: There have been many pet holiday cards, but my favorites have been the ones featuring Sadie, my dog. Sadie is very cooperative and has been photographed sitting in Santa's lap (at a holiday party for pets given by her vet), and in front of the fireplace wearing fleece doggie pajamas while waiting for Santa. One photo was simply a close-up of Sadie's delicately crossed front paws — when you look closely at the photo you can see that her toenails had been painted red and green. (Don't worry — I removed the polish immediately and then washed her feet.)

Q: Like Flora, I know you like to make presents as much as receiving them. What are some of your favorite presents that you've made?

A: For years now I've made holiday outfits for the kids in my life — my nephew, godchildren, friends' children, cousins' children. Most of the outfits feature smocking for the girls and younger children, but I also have fun knitting sweaters, hats, and scarves. I start planning my holiday stitching in August every year, because it takes so long to make everything. I look forward to my autumn sewing all year long.

Is it possible to have two best friends?

Main Street

#4: Best Friends | Ann M. Martin

When Flora finds out that her old best friend is coming to visit her, Flora's excited—but her new best friend, Olivia, isn't. Olivia's afraid she won't measure up. Is there room for two best friends or will Flora have to make a choice?